I0457754

LISSY

Elaine Balliet

DOHENY and LORDEN

California

DOHENY and LORDEN

Los Angeles, California

This book is a work of fiction. Names, characters, places, and incidents either are products of the author's imagination or are used fictitiously. Any resemblance to actual events or locales or persons, living or dead, is entirely coincidental.

Copyright 2012 by Elaine Balliet

All rights reserved. No part of this book may be reproduced in any form without the permission of Doheny and Lorden and the author.

Printed in the United States of America

ISBN 13: 978-0615608020

Library of Congress Catalog Number 2012934338

For Roo

Contents

My dearest Lissy,

In just four days, you'll start school. I know you're hoping for a car, but I'll still be driving you to the bus stop at least for awhile. I think you'll like what I've been up to these past few days. Although they don't need it, I washed your sheets and your comforter, too. I was thinking about getting you a new one, but the old one still fits so well with the décor and looks so good upon your bed and I know how much you like it anyway. Today I bought you this new potpourri that smells like the islands and placed it in these pretty little sachets throughout your room, the two of us will have to get back there someday soon. And, I bought you that new jacket that you've wanted for school and hung it where you can see it when you get in. I think you'll like it; it's that gray one with the soft hood, and pockets on the inside.

I can't wait until you get here, because there's so much that I want to tell you. Like how much I love you and I've missed you, and how there's this one deer that keeps on coming down to the garden, a doe, it must be the lavender flowers that are attracting her to the vines. I know that the river is a little low this season, which is why your father and I are going to place an old tub in the garden for a trough so that she can drink while she's here. With hunting season almost upon us, and as summer turns to fall, she will be gone soon enough. She has a small scar above her eye and the cutest flecks of white upon her tail. She's curious and bold, and I find myself worrying about her with the coming hunting season. Deer aren't common here at all, which is why I find it highly unusual for her to be frequenting the garden. She seems to want something, if she could only talk.

I drove down to Austin yesterday, past the old house and your old school. Although it's been a little over a year since we moved, it seems like yesterday. Nothing's changed, but then again, I didn't expect it to. The house still looks the same, except that the white shutters we had in the windows are now vanilla mini blinds and our blue stone driveway is Spanish pavers. But it feels the same, like you and I and daddy are still inside. Lissy, I'm so sorry for the move. I know how much living there and having your friends close meant to you. I wish we could go back in time, I really do.

Before I headed back, I went by the high school to say hello to some of the teachers who taught you, especially Mrs. Marpole. She asked about you and how you were doing and if you still liked to study before dinner and when she did, her eyes lit up like it was the first day of school, like she knew something I didn't, some secret, and maybe she does. I know how much you liked her; she hasn't changed a bit since she taught you, her hair is still piled high atop her head and she was wearing one of her trademark long dresses and a funny pair of shoes. She made every day special, and you just don't find too many teachers like her anymore.

I gave her some sachets that I filled and a few packets of morning glory seeds so that she can enjoy the hummingbirds too, and when I drove away over the bridge and left her and the city behind, I was so sad that I cried. I miss Austin, Lissy, like you do. You might think I don't, but I do. We were happier there and your father was, too. It was casual, fun, preppy, with a real artsy feel, but at the same time laid-

2

back, the opposite of where we took you to. But sometimes, for whatever reason, life takes you down that different row. And it's up to us to make the best of it wherever we are, whatever we do.

On the drive back, as I left the bridge behind, this past year and everything that's happened was weighing on my mind, so I pulled off the road and parked for awhile. And that's when I got to thinking about everything that's wrong with the world, and everything that's right, too, and how, no matter how happy or sad that we're feeling, or how much we don't want it to, that the sun will always shine. There'll always be a new day to wake up to, no matter what city we're in, no matter how much distance is between us, no matter how sick or healthy we are, no matter what. And that new day brings with it a new dawn and the promise of a new us- to accomplish or not to accomplish, to learn or not to learn, to love or not to love, to laugh harder than we have ever laughed before, to hug our children and parents, to walk a little taller and to catch a falling star. With us or without us, the world will go on.

So we hug each other a little tighter, kiss each other a little longer, say 'I love you,' just one more time, treat our fellow man with kindness and rise with the dawn, in the hope that just a little of that promise will rub off on us, and we'll rise that day and the next to see another hummingbird and to laugh beneath the stars. We do what we can when we can with what we have until we're gone. And if we spread a little love and sunshine along our path, it will blossom tenfold.

I guess that's all that I really wanted to say right now, Lissy, except that I love you and I always will.

All my love,

Mom.

Swing

As guns sound somewhere off the Mexico/Texas border and the shrapnel rains down, another innocent life succumbs to the drug war crimes as Lissy swings. She could be anybody's daughter but she's not, she's Steven and Marie's, an only child of willow frame, safflower hair and almond eyes, not quite 17 and severely addicted to cocaine.

It was yesterday nearly two decades ago on a seasonably hot, humid day, when Lissy was born in the nondescript but artsy town of Austin nine months into a non-eventful pregnancy. It was July in the summer of '93, as Lissy, officially christened Elizabeth Desiree Harrington Boman, entered the world that day. Harrington was her mother's maiden name; Boman, the name that Steven had given Marie upon marriage. The middle name of 'Desiree' had been borrowed from a favorite aunt on Steven's side of the family.

With a circle of family waiting impatiently outside the Austin delivery room she entered the world with a perfunctory shriek- healthy, buoyant, bright, fair, and free- all 7.5 pounds, and more importantly, *not* addicted to methamphetamine as she is today. Another nameless face is thrown into another unmarked grave as Lissy swings, and Marie is thankful that she hasn't had a 3 a.m. call, and that her only daughter survived another night on the streets, for she prays that she did, at least. Her parents stay strong on the glimmer in her almond eyes- a light that is dark, wild, and deep, deep as her cry in the delivery room that July, Austin day, strength that gives her parents reason to believe.

Her lungs fill with air as the gathering outside the delivery room gives thanks for the miracle of birth, and for the miracle of everything. And it's all okay, as Lissy wails and the miracle of birth is reveled in. As the cord is cut, she is held lovingly, nuzzled within a mother's love as only a mother's love is and can be. But it isn't the summer of 93, and somewhere in Ciudad, Juarez, a child lies bleeding on the streets.

Perhaps the hardest part is coming to terms with accepting that this was the way that it is, that this is reality, and in trying to make sense of the tragedy that had become Lissy's life, and her parent's lives, and sorting through the pain. There is no safe place, no sleep, and no peace when a child is in a life or death battle with drugs, and has become hopelessly addicted to cocaine. As Marie cries, her ribs contract in pain, and she covers her face with Lissy's pillow in efforts to hear the swing.

The backyard swing creaks that summer of '98, as Marie and Steven's bouncing baby girl grows happier and healthier by the day, squealing with a child's joy, flailing her limbs free. Back and forth she swings, giggling as her mother gives her another push, her legs dragging in the cool earth beneath.

"Higher, mommy," she calls, lifting her feet. "I want to be as high as the birds and the trees. I can do it. I'm five finally."

Laughing like children do, she pushes higher in the warm, Texas breeze as her mother fades away beneath.

"Five more minutes, Lissy," Marie says. "Because it's getting late and we need to get Daddy's dinner ready. We'll come back here tomorrow; besides, you know how much you love hot dogs all rolled up in bread, anyway."

"Pigs in a blanket!" Lissy screams, her face lighting up bigger and brighter than the Austin sky.

"My favorite, mommy! I can't believe that you made my favorite thing!"

Refusing to heed her mother, she swings until the sun fades behind the tall oak trees, content in her childish ways, aware of only what the swing has to offer. And then the swing fades, as the Austin summer does to the winter rain.

But it isn't that summer of 98, or that carefree afternoon in the family yard, but just another heartbreaking day, as Marie chokes down a Valium, followed by bourbon, in her garden full of only seeds. Stabbing the soil with a hoe, her mind drifts and she hears the swing, as a dozen young men are tortured, then beheaded in Ciudad, Juarez, 100 yards beyond the bridge that connects the border town to El Paso.

Lissy is alive, she's a smart girl, and she'll come back to me.

Steven and Marie pray, down on their knees, in the nearby parish of St. Justin Martyr, as the entire community of El Paso prays for Lissy that day, just like every other day. The grief too much too bear, Marie accidently stabs her finger instead of the dirt beneath.

If she is still alive, Steven and Marie will be among the lucky ones, as 50,000 mothers and fathers arrange for the digging of 50,000 graves, for sons and daughters who have met their deaths in Juarez and just outside, ever since the escalation of the drug wars in December of 2006. Yet, in spite of all the tragedy and senseless killings, the war over drugs rages on and more innocent children die, by overdose from their drug of choice, or murdered in the streets. Strong in their faith, Steven and Marie keep alive the hope that their only child breathes...

Desperate, alone, strung out on cocaine, strung out on anything and everything- in need of a fix and questioning another nameless face; not caring if she lives or dies, yet they still have faith, because there's absolutely nothing that they or anyone else can do about it, which is why Lissy swings. With every breath that they take, Steven and Marie believe. In love, in life, in the power of prayer and hope over Lissy's addiction to cocaine.

Before the events of the past 24 months had transpired, Steven and Marie had never given a thought to drugs or to addiction, it had never entered the picture that was their daughter's life, as Lissy stepped from the swing to the top of her class and valedictorian of her freshman class at El Paso High in the summer of '07. That was the year in which her drug abuse began, the year that her parents made the decision to move to the ranch in El Paso that Lissy's father had inherited from a brother earlier that spring. Although they wanted to believe otherwise, the unfortunate relocation from Austin to El Paso had everything to do with their only child's drug addiction, and downhill spiral with cocaine. Whether there was anything different that Steven and Marie could have done still remains unanswered, even after all of the time and the pain.

Marie reaches down to plant another morning glory seed and smiles, flattening a small mound of dirt over the seed. Lissy had a special affection for morning glories, which is why she was planting, and which made her wonder how a girl who was so smart- class valedictorian, song leader, and president of the debate team could do a 100% turn around to becoming dependent upon cocaine. The Lissy that her parents had known up until the end of her freshman year was a morning glory herself, a flake of snow, a butterfly in the first light of day. As Marie patted the earth over the fragile seeds, she determinedly celebrated Lissy's 17th birthday and victory over her disease.

Somewhere, right now, somehow, here in El Paso alongside the River Rio Grande, irrespective of the river stones and muddy water, a newly-bloomed morning glory grows wild and free.

Her parents placed the blame for Lissy's drug abuse on the move, and to the day that they took ownership of the deed and of the sprawling ranch along the river just at the Mexican border of Juarez. It was spring, and Lissy was almost 15. To the teens at El Paso High School, crossing the crumbled concrete bridge into the Mexican border city was a risky game, even before the drug wars started, with the resulting deaths and violence in and around the city. Yet when they had made the decision to move, there had been no gunfire at night, no violence or drug lords roaming the streets, just long stretches of fertile evergreen ranch land that housed two hundred head of longhorn cattle and beckoned with towering ancient Texas oak trees. Even after their acceptance of her addiction and dependence, the resulting problems seemed surreal, were surreal, to Steven and Marie. Yet considering the alternative, surreal wasn't such a bad place to be.

It's the end of summer in the small, artsy, town of El Paso and Marie is preparing for another day's work in the gallery, and it's time to ready the barn for the winter again, not time to be planting the beloved morning glories, because the heat and humidity of the desert make it difficult for them to take hold in the dry earth beneath. The Mexican police and *federales,* after the election of President Felipe, have finally taken the initiative to remove the drug cartels from the Juarez streets. And Lissy, despite her life-threatening addiction, had finally been taking little steps in the direction of conquering her thirst for cocaine. Yet, like the morning glories from seed, those steps were unable to stay. Over and over again, the move is blamed, as is her parent's failure to stop anything, everything.

Questions are tossed back and forth among the family and the community, questions such as *"How could this happen to our Lissy? To the only child of the family? Beloved daughter of a hard-working and dedicated, physician father and loving wife and mother?"*

Her parents, just like all the other parents of addicted sons and daughters everywhere, were sure that they had done everything right over the years of raising their family; at least, that's what they believed.

How does addiction happen to any family? How does addiction happen to our family?

Over and over Steven and Marie, and the community of El Paso asked these things. Yet, rich or poor, of superior intellect or not, any child who uses any addictive drug or crack cocaine *even once* is at risk for a life-threatening and relentless addiction from the cravings it creates. In Lissy's case, the damage had been inflicted silently and painlessly, the months racing through her veins, the poison ravaging her system until she was empty, save for the hatred and rage that she had for her family for moving her out of Austin and away from her friends in the first place.

Praying for rain in the desert heat and for a miracle, Marie pats just a little more earth over the seeds before turning back to the lonesome ranch house that, up until Lissy's addiction, had been the family home.

– – –

It's been 21 days of prayers and heat since the last day of Lissy's sophomore year and since they've heard any word, which could mean anything. Prostitution, incarceration, illness, overdose, death- all come to mind when they pictured her on the streets. After another pill and swig of bourbon, Marie sees the elusive swing clearly- the girl with the long, safflower hair that blows in the warm Texas air sailing back and forth, wild and free from cocaine.

A phone call, a letter maybe. Anything to prove that she breathes.

In her easy place, Marie plants the seeds, but it had been too many days with no word and tonight marked the beginning of the third week. It terrified Marie that while working in the garden in an effort to ease her fears and pain, or while doing any chore to take her mind off things, that her precious baby girl could be prostituting herself for drugs or money in the midst of a country where death didn't mean anything, a country on the brink of a civil war.

Was she warm? Was she thinking of them? Negotiating a trade of the jacket upon her back for drugs or money? Caught in the crossfire of the streets? Lying in a puddle of her blood, maybe?

Addiction begins with the little things. As a child growing up in the suburban city of Austin, Lissy had loved steak. Peppering it and smothering it in lots of ketchup, she would devour it instantly. Yet, prior to her disappearance, Lissy became violently ill if she ate steak or any form of meat. In that winter of Lissy's 15th year in '93, the addiction left her esophagus ruined, and unable to digest any form of meat. As the little girl on the swing called to Marie, a frightened but defiant Lissy disappeared to inject cocaine into a vein.

I'm in that happy place again, but the swing doesn't creak. Why doesn't it creak?

Gazing up at the swing, a weak smile upon her face, Marie brushed away a tear as she pushed the seat which fades into morning glory seeds. Lilac morning glories, Lissy's very favorite kind. But the ground is parched, dry, in need of rain.

The air will be cool again very soon, winter- Lissy's favorite time of year, and her favorite flowers will still be in bloom, perennial, victorious of the cocaine and the Texas heat.

Hurtling another plate at Marie, Lissy vomits violently and the lilac flowers fade away.

Before this last disappearance, Lissy, at 5' 3," had weighed in at a healthy 115 and had remained sober for 15 days, thrilled that she had finally put on some weight. Yet addiction and cocaine is a silent, slithering, snake. Digging its fangs in, it pierce's its victim's skin with poison, taking hold of mind and body, and doesn't release. Knowing what they know now after months of exhaustive education on the disease, Steven and Marie finally understand why Lissy had never been successful in keeping her weight.

As the seeds wither in the heat, Marie's heart becomes heavy, yet she continues to pat the ground after dabbing water on her face. Seven hours in the garden and 110 degrees on a seasonably hot, El Paso day was a lifetime away from the winter that Lissy turned 16. Somewhere between her freshman year and the time that she had blown out the 16 candles upon her cake, Steven and Marie's baby girl had graduated from the top of her class to a common addict of the streets. After accepting her award, she had hurriedly left the ceremony to meet up with friends to score some methamphetamine across the bridge in Ciudad. Steven and Marie knew this because Steven had taken the liberty of reading Lissy's text messages that evening after a scare two weeks prior had sent them to an El Paso emergency room. Lissy had suffered another nosebleed, one which wasn't going away, after stumbling through the door early in the morning from another secretive place.

That was another 'little' thing, the nosebleeds. Another 'little' thing was that methamphetamine and crack cocaine was the hardest drug to kick with the exception of heroin, another 'little' thing that Steven and Marie had learned by way of their education on the consequences of the disease. As far as they were concerned that winter of 93, it was the devil that had come to prey, selecting their child to torment as they helplessly watched her bleed.

Escaping to that happy place, Marie breathes in the serenity, trying to rationalize Lissy's addiction once again as she thinks about the disease. The tragic thing was that they hadn't any ammunition left- they had tried everything. In the disease process, the addict wasn't the only one affected, the entire family falls victim as well, until there is no one left to save. The devil spared no one in his evil game.

Lifting the lid on the big, antique trunk in Lissy's bedroom, Marie removes a letter to read, 21 letters for 21 days, a letter from a stack of letters that Marie has written, letters that Lissy one day might be alive to read. A letter that won't end up covered in the dust of a family's shattered dreams. The day when their daughter would come home for good and the battle would be behind them and the devil would sleep. Like the swing, the letters are therapy for the pain, as Marie takes pen to paper to write again.

The sun sets upon the sprawling dwelling that Steven and Marie no longer call home along the riverbed, the dwelling in El Paso alongside the lazy and meandering Rio Grande, as another child is introduced to cocaine. Somewhere, on some poorly-lit street, in the dust and the heat, Lissy calls out to their dreams.

States

Addiction isn't something that happens overnight, no one sets out to be an addict, a vagrant, an alcoholic, a thief. Steven, like any other shattered and tortured father, was working late at the office again, which was okay. Like Marie's garden, it was therapy.

Staring out through the picture window of the ranch's spacious front room, Marie's toes poked the creamy carpet as her eyes roamed the street. Like the night before, and the night before that, nothing was there, no sound of childish footfall through the weeds, only the occasional feline which prowled the darkened street.

Most nights since Lissy's disappearance, Steven and Marie would sit and drink while staring blankly, waiting for the sound of girlish laughter, or for the knock of a night-duty cop who would tell them that their daughter had been discovered dead upon a Juarez street. With methodical sips, they attempted to ease away the pain, listening for the footfall that never came.

Over the months of Lissy's struggles with addiction, they poured their hearts into becoming experts on her disease, in an effort to uncover the 'whys' behind her addictive and defiant behavior. An art consultant for a local gallery, a year into her daughter's disease, Marie requested a much needed absence to try to fathom why her daughter had allowed the odorless white powder to ravage her mind and body, destroying her being in the reasoning that addiction was okay.

Show me an angel who neither sins nor sleeps, and I'll show you someone who has never breathed.

After months of endless substance abuse classes spent listening to addicts in all stages of recovery tell their stories, Marie learned that an addict like Lissy was in a helpless state, one which forbade any involvement in normal activity. School, the gym, the movies, the beach, a dinner out- all ceased in the name of cocaine. As much as Lissy wanted to change, she just couldn't help it- the addiction had taken over, and that's just the way it was. Now, 'normal' was anything but- nausea, a headache, acne, vomiting, a stomach ache.

Cocaine abuse begins innocently- recreational drug use on the weekend, but no matter how 'innocently' it begins, addiction is where it leads. So after months of education on drug use and abuse, and after learning what they could on the tragic effects of their daughter's disease, Steven and Marie finally realized that it was futile to sit back and wait for their daughter to ask for help or to acknowledge her lack of control over her disease, which was the day they decided to make Lissy's addiction their life's mission, because nothing about it was okay. Only the backing of their close friends and their pastor kept them from giving up entirely.

In the front room, as they drank, beneath a cushion of the sofa, they discovered another needle cap, small and orange, which Lissy had forgotten to throw away.

Out of love for Lissy, and for the person they knew their daughter really was, deep down inside, and by participating in discussions and by educating themselves on methamphetamine, it was their sincere hope and belief that if they were just in possession of the right weapons, they would win the battle- one day. While their daughter was powerless to her disease, they were able to help. Their love for their daughter, combined with the ongoing support and education, provided them with the strength and courage to fight the snake. Possibly the most valuable lesson they learned and what keeps them going is that if there's life, there's hope, regardless of the addiction or the pain. If they were to bring their only child back, there was no other way to think.

There's a corner of the front room that still bears a vomit stain from one of Lissy's bouts with the 'flu,' and which will have to be professionally cleaned before the new owners take over the ranch after the close of escrow in six weeks. Where they move isn't as important as their need to get away. From the river's edge through the open shutters there's the hint of a cooling Texas breeze, as they fall together to stare out into the yard past the porch, where the For Sale sign creaks, like the swing.

After she had vomited that morning, Lissy's balance had become unsteady and she had suffered another nose bleed before collapsing. Because it was just too painful to see their daughter so critically ill and under the influence, Steven had punched his fist through another wall and Marie had hung her head in grief. The next morning, along with patching the wall, they did what they did every day, which was to worry if Lissy was going to die, or be okay.

Fix

"It's going to be dark soon, Liss. Just this once, let's score back in town. I don't care about the cost, I'll pay the diff."

Scuttling beneath a rusted barbed wire fence, he removed a barb which had become lodged in the hood of her jacket. Rubbing the site of the puncture to remove the rust which was accumulating there did no good, as the hole which the barb had created only grew larger. The poverty-stricken border town, for all intense purposes, was dead, and there was a chill to the air. Shivering, he pulled his coat a little closer to his neck as he prodded her again.

"Name the price, I don't care. I just want to get the heck out of here."

His words lost to the air, they approached the bridge as she glared at him again.

"Hey," he continued. "I don't know about you, but I don't feel like being down here."

He could think of a hundred places he'd like to be after graduating from class that afternoon, but Juarez wasn't one of them. Although it was only 4 p.m., dusk was settling in as the dampness and cold grew stronger.

"This place makes me nervous, Liss."

Glancing around nervously, his eyes rested on the dilapidated shacks, plywood and cardboard cutouts of another era, one far removed from the affluent urban neighborhood in which they both lived in El Paso. But deep down inside he knew that she didn't care.

He had known the girl with the safflower hair which hung down past her waist ever since the beginning of their freshman year, when she had moved into El Paso and the sprawling ranch house along the riverbed, and it hadn't taken long before they had become best friends, inseparable, almost. That was, when she wasn't taking advantage of him again. Tired of arguing, he put his head in his hands and sat down in the muddy grass growing out from the bridge and the water's edge. He couldn't believe that he had let her talk him into this. It was his fault that they were down here. He should have listened to his conscience.

"Cluck, cluck, *Chicken*!" Lissy said, placing a foot on the bridge and taunting him again. "Leave me here then, I'll go alone, I'm not scared. I can't believe you're chicken, Trev! I expected a little more from you, and you let me down. Again!"

Flipping back her hair, she stood defiantly upon the broken step.

The way that she was standing there, one slender, tanned leg poised on the bridge, and one off of it, made him wish that they were more than just friends. And the way that the waning sunlight played off her shoulders made him want to pick her up in his arms and dance. He had always wanted her, yet like the gentleman that he was, had never made his thoughts known to her, or said anything which might lead her to believe that he cared.

"It's four in the afternoon," she continued, kicking at the step playfully as her eyes met his. "It isn't dark, we're American citizens and live directly across the border on the other side of this old piece of shit, and besides, we have passports. Even if something happens, which it won't, they can't keep us here. Trust me on this one, Trev."

As always, she was insistent in her disobedience. Defiant, her eyes narrowed in like the silent chilled air between them.

"What is this world coming to if I can't count on you, Trev? You know, sometimes, you can be a real bitch, and I'm sick of it."

As she glared at him and placed her hands on her hips, he bit his lip, drawing blood, as she began arguing again.

"I can't believe you're thinking of turning back after all of this effort. When I met you, you weren't afraid of anything, and look at you now, afraid of the air. Nothing's going to happen to us here, I promise. We'll score enough meth to keep us high for a couple of weeks and then we won't come back- ever. We'll do it your way, try another place, somewhere 'safe,'" she taunted, eyes burned into his.

She certainly enjoyed teasing him, it was even better than her favorite pizza with extra cheese piled high upon it.

"Cluck, cluck, *Chicken*! Have you ever seen the Chicken dance, Trev? You put your hands on your hips and then you shake it like this."

Placing her hands on her hips, she shook her hips and clucked.

As he laughed, he thought about crossing. She was right, they did live right across the border, and the sun was still high above the horizon. By the time it set, they would have scored the meth, and would be safely back in El Paso and far away from the evils of Juarez. With her flowing blonde

24

hair and feminine wiles, Lissy had lots of connections south of the bridge.

"Cluck, cluck, cluck, *Chicken*! Come on, Trevor! I promise on my life that this is the last time that I'll drag you down here. If I come down here again, I'll bring that boy who you despise that was in our English class- remember? The one that combs his hair the entire time that he's sitting there, while he looks at himself in the mirror?"

Ah, Preston, he remembered him well, he did. All 6 ft and 4" of him. And she was right, he disliked him intensely, although the feeling of absolute loath for the running back of the football team and complete dissatisfaction with him hadn't really started until he had called him out on the fact that he continually stared at Liss, and that he continued to stare, even after he knew that it was really bothering him. Parked on his athletic and tight rear on the far side of the classroom, he never took his eyes off her the entire time that they were in the classroom. Even Professor Hornton had noticed it, an old coot who couldn't tell his front from his rear. Ah, Preston. He only had eyes for Liss. As he thought of him now, his hands clenched into a fist, as he kicked at the cracked pavement.

"You know how well that you two get along," she said in jest, as he gritted his teeth and kept his eyes fastened on hers. "I was even thinking of asking him to be my boyfriend next year. So there."

"Preston, oh Preston, can I wear your jacket?" she laughed, ignoring him to begin crossing over. "Do you think that he will make a good kisser, Trevor?"

Instead of fearful, now he was mad, his fists tightening into rocks again. More than any other girl, or anyone, for that matter, Lissy really knew how to get to him. The handsome, stocky quarterback with the buzzed head had had the attention of not just Lissy, but of every girl who had ever attended El Paso High from its initiation. Now, more than ever, her taunting and threats were getting to him.

"From now on we'll get our meth and crack in Laredo," she said, teetering across the concrete with her back to him. "It's nowhere near as pure, but it'll do."

Blowing him a kiss, she pretended to take a hit.

"Come on, chicken boy, just one more time for your Lissy."

If there was one thing that Lissy was, along with being downright gorgeous, it was insistent. It didn't matter a dime what he thought or cared, because it didn't matter to her. With a last look behind him, he sighed and got up from the grass, as Lissy continued to place distance between them. The late afternoon air cold on his neck, he pulled at the hood of his jacket.

"You say that now, but I know you better than that, Liss," he said, trying to wipe the grass stains from his pants. "You know as well as I do that the second you run out of crack and are dope sick again, that you'll be begging me to come back down here to Juarez. You don't listen to me, Liss. You never have, you never will, and for what it's worth, I think this little trip down here was ridiculous. I can tell you over and over again how dangerous I think it is, but you don't listen, and you don't care. Just for once I wish you'd listen, Liss."

Catching up to walk alongside her, he continued to wipe his pants, more out of nervousness than an attempt to keep the stains from setting in.

Being crowned valedictorian of her freshman class less than an hour ago had given her a high, but it wasn't the kind of high she craved, because she had already moved on to 'better' things, those which were over the bridge. Exasperated, he kept pace beside her as they crossed over into Juarez. Heart pounding, he bit down hard on his tongue, drawing blood again. He had to agree with her that the meth that they were after gave you a high that kept you riding for hours, a high that you couldn't get anywhere; he and Lissy were living proof of that. Life was good, and so was the potent and sugary powder from Juarez.

"Who are we meeting up with? You never told me that?"

As long as it wasn't Pitch, he didn't care. Keeping his calm so that he wouldn't keep biting his tongue, he trudged along with her through the thick grass which grew out from the chunks of concrete, overtaking it. The ugly town near deserted, a small group of kids bounced a lopsided ball beside some dirty shacks.

Last time they had scored down here, it was from a stocky, shifty-eyed fellow with a missing thumb, the one who went by the name of Pitch. Thinking back, he couldn't help but wonder how he had gotten the name to begin with. Something to do with the missing digit, no doubt. Some things were just better left unsaid. Thinking of Pitch and his missing thumb, and the hideous tattoos that littered his scarred chest gave him the shivers like no other. The Mexican bandit even had a pair of eyeballs tattooed on the back of his neck. Wondering if Lissy felt the chill like he did, he yanked at the jacket again. A light cotton windbreaker, he would have done as well without it.

"I hope we're not hooking up with Pitch, Liss. Not only don't I trust him, but he gives me the creeps and makes me want to vomit. What kind of guy would tattoo eyes on the back of his neck?"

This part about Pitch, along with his name, really worried him.

"It isn't Pitch, Trev," Lissy answered. "So feel better. Someone named Raul has the meth, and he comes recommended from the best."

Her tone had turned sarcastic and she had become insistent again. Her returning sarcasm should have made him feel better, but it didn't, as he watched a dirty kid, a girl of about 10, kick the ball high into the air. Bouncing off one of the flimsy cardboard shacks, it knocked one wall to the earth, as an old woman with even older hair, sporting a clenched fist shuffled out, shaking it towards them, the kids flying off in separate directions.

"You can't judge a man by his tattoos, Trevor. Or by his neck. You should know that."

Not one to be fearful, Lissy grinned broadly.

"I'll give you that," he said. "But together, they make a strange statement, one which I haven't figured out yet."

Just then, the old woman disappeared back into the shack.

"Besides, I thought that Raul was found dead in a ditch out in the middle of nowhere."

Just mentioning his name sent the shivers up him again.

"Wasn't it some kind of overdose, Liss? I think that I remember you telling me that."

"Raul's just fine, you're thinking of Snitch. It was Snitch they found at the bottom of that canyon behind the hills outside of Juarez last winter, Trevor."

Stupid Trevor. Thinking of how ridiculous he really was, she kicked at a stick. He was causing her to doubt herself, like he always did. With a snort, she laughed. Trevor was such a spoilsport.

"Actually, when you think about it," she continued, "it's kind of ironic. He beat up kids that snitched, but he himself was a snitch. Can you just picture it, being tortured? I won't tell you what he looked like when they found him, but poor Snitch."

Hearing what had happened to Snitch certainly didn't make him feel any better.

As if to mock him, she laughed, tossing back strands of silky hair which shone in the last rays of the sun.

If Trevor kept wasting time with all of these stupid questions, it *would* grow dark while they were down here, and even she didn't want that, although she would never let on to him.

"Look, we're meeting up with Raul any sec, so loosen up. He's never tortured any kid. Especially a white kid. At least I don't think so."

29

Her almond eyes dim as the light around them, he bit his tongue again. Maybe Lissy was right, and he really was turning into a wuss.

"If he had, you wouldn't know. That's just it."

He wasn't convinced. All he knew was that it was growing colder by the second and that they shouldn't be down here.

"Why do you think these guys go by fake names, Liss? They don't want to get caught. This dope had better be worth the hassle of coming all the way down here, I'll say that." Removing a wad of tissue from a pocket, he wiped at the blood which had appeared, then stuffed it back in.

They had been traveling on the desolate street for the better part of an hour, with not a soul in sight, save for the lone kid or transient every now and then. Juarez wasn't a place you wanted to be after dark. Not even if you were Mexican. The dilapidated wooden shacks had evolved into cardboard, which was really bothering him, and there was a funny smell to the air. Stifling a cough, he tried to conceal his fear, as she walked alongside him, kicking at a stray bottle or can every now and then.

"Don't you ever get scared, Lissy? Just look around us. Those dirty kids, see how they stare? Maybe we shouldn't be doing this."

The narrow street they were walking down had lost all traces of cement and had turned to dirt, until even the cardboard houses disappeared and the final rays of sun went down behind them, as the shadows set in and he kicked a can in frustration. He wasn't going to admit it, but he was downright disappointed. Where was this fellow Raul, anyway? Why hadn't Lissy been more specific with him as to the arrangements of their meeting? Sometimes she really made him mad, which made him wonder why they were even friends.

"Where is he, Lissy?"

As he spoke, two dark and silent figures emerged from the darkened grass on the path, shrouded in a veil of smoke. Smoke he knew only too well by the scent. Meth might be what they were after, but the smell of good hash he couldn't resist as he closed his eyes and inhaled a long, deep breath. Glancing over his shoulder, he watched as the pair disappeared across the path into another tall clump of grass. Trying to ignore his mounting fear, he took hold of her hand.

"Say, can this dude Raul score us some hash so that we can smoke a bowl before we get high on meth, Liss? We'll have a trip that we'll never forget, and you know how you like it. Let's make this trip down here worth it. I told my folks that I was spending the night at Tory's again, and I wouldn't be surprised if they called me out on it."

"You're 16, Trevor, and your folks still check up? How rude!"

Her voice had become strained and the two figures were back, walking parallel to them through the grass about ten yards back from the path, and she prayed that Trevor wouldn't notice.

Where was Raul, anyways?

Even the sight of the wary Mexican would ease her mounting fear. She would never let on to Trevor, but she was scared. Raul had been supposed to meet them an hour ago back at the bridge. Since they were well beyond it, how much farther down this seedy road would they have to tread in hopes of finding him? As the shadows grew and the grass dimmed, someone coughed in the settling dusk. Trembling, but not showing it, she attacked Trevor again.

"You're not an infant; you're going to be a junior next year. I'm sure that Raul has our stash, and that he'll be here. I've heard that he has everything, and we don't have a reason not to trust him. Don't I always make it worth it, Trev? Every time we come down here? We'll smoke some hash, take some hits, and then we'll head back. Before you know it, you'll be safe and sound in your own little bed, wishing you and I were down here!"

She was actually right, he'd give her that, and she was giving him that look again, a look which said that one day they might be more than just friends. He could only wish. More coughing erupted from the shadows, coughing that he heard, as he sucked in his breath and looked around them.

"We should have brought my dad's gun," he said, as a bat flew past them. "Not the rifle, but the '45. Having a gun for protection would make us feel better, Liss."

He couldn't speak for her, but he would be one young puppy who would feel a lot better if he had his hot little hand 'round the smooth, polished shaft of one of his father's guns.

"Lissy? Did you hear what I said? Or are you ignoring me again?"

If Lissy didn't like what she heard, she played deaf. It was one of her tricks.

"Yes, I guess we could have thought of it. Your father's gun?" she said mockingly. "Now that's a brilliant idea, Trev, because then we'd be down here in jail. Hey, don't ever apply to be a rocket scientist, because they won't let you in."

"Well, I think that we need something to protect us. Things happen, Liss. Even with the best made plans."

"Because things might happen is why I should be scared?" she answered. "Ha! You know me better than that."

The dusty path was teeming with bats as a shot rang out in the darkness.

Trevor was annoying, in one of his moods, and she shouldn't have brought him here. And now to make matters worse, her stomach hurt again.

"I don't feel good, Trevor, my stomach hurts."

It really did hurt, because the pains were kicking in. Pains which came from the use of, then lack of, cocaine or meth. Pains which signified that she needed to quit.

"You just need to shoot up. We both do, Lissy. It's why we're at each other's throats, and it's why we're here."

Thinking about how good they were going to feel when they finally shot up some really good stuff made him laugh.

"Is that Raul?" he whispered, as a shadow appeared from behind a shack. "But this guy is tall, Liss."

"No, I don't think so. Raul isn't as tall as that. From the description that I was given of him, that guy doesn't fit."

With a deep sigh, she pushed back her hair.

What if they were ambushed out in this nowhere pile of shit and left for dead? Would anyone even think to look for them down here?

Cradling the wad of cash in her pants, she shoved it in further. Considering Trevor's fear, it was time to lighten things up a bit.

"Double dare, Trev, and I go first. I double dare you, Trevor Joe Mansfield, to follow me back to Raul's place, wherever it is, after we score to shoot up. With him. He'll appreciate our show of friendship, I'm sure, and he no doubt gets high himself, so are you up to it? I double dare you, Trev!"

Her very best friend in the whole wide world was becoming a real wuss and it couldn't last.

"I'm sure he's an alright guy," she said. "And besides, if we cut him in on a few extra bucks…"

This was it; she had reached the point of no return and hit the fence, giving him no choice other than to butt heads.

"And then what, Liss? We all live happily ever after and become best buds and all that? Ask Raul to join us back in El Paso? Invite him to Sunday dinner even? I don't think so, Lissy, not a chance. He'll pretend he's our friend, and then one time when we're all together, when we don't have our guard up, he'll introduce us to his homeboys and they'll steal our cash. Maybe they'll even knock us off, as an extra benefit. You really do need to shoot up, Liss. Come to think of it, so do I."

Now, he felt sick, as he stared hard through the darkness past the lone dingy shack. Like Lissy's, he had begun having stomach problems his freshman year, and they were still continuing.

The street was dark, with the only light an hour or more back across the border to Juarez. In his opinion, things were getting worse by the minute.

"How far are we going to keep walking? We should have borrowed a car or taken a cab."

"There are no cabs that will come into Juarez anymore, Trev. A car? Maybe. But it's too late for that. Besides, I'll have my license next month, finally. What about you?"

As she rambled, he couldn't help but notice that her almond eyes had turned a pale shade of "pick on Trev" again, as he discussed his prized mode of transportation.

"I have one; you know that, we're just waiting for the wheels. The renovation of the old Mustang's almost finished, I think I already told you awhile back. I'll never be able to thank my father enough for saving it from the junkyard, Liss. He's really done a number on it."

A clunker no longer, the 1967 Fastback that they had been working on for the better part of a year finally had all of the kinks out of it and all of the pieces were finally coming together, including two precision coats of avocado-green, high gloss, metallic paint. Yep, his new set of wheels was now a real charmer and chick-mobile, and was almost ready to roll down the streets of El Paso, and out on past.

"Well, aren't we cool? Should have, could have, didn't," she said, glaring again.

She was now not just on his nerves, but under his skin. Like a cherished and comfy blanket which now had fleas on it. Yes, that was Lissy lately, just one big bad itch.

"Five more minutes, Liss, and if he hasn't shown, I'm turning around. We'll come back down here tomorrow, I promise. You have my word on it."

He had started coughing again, and the nervousness had settled in. Maybe he was imagining it, but one of the shanty kids had just spit at them. Since Lissy was taunting him, he might as well join the party. Throwing the shanty kid a dirty look, he laughed.

"Valedictorian of her freshman class at El Paso High School. Now, isn't that a special honor. I'm not trying to make you feel bad, Lissy, or burst your bubble, but El Paso High isn't exactly up there on the list of schools which are top notch academically."

"Really? she answered. "Then *you* claim the title then, which wouldn't happen in a million years, Trev. Because, academically speaking, you're just not all there."

Ignoring the hurtful comment, he made small talk as they walked past the shacks. If Raul didn't show any second, he was out of here.

"What made your folks move down here anyways, Liss? You don't fit in here, you never did. Your hair, clothes, perfume, your tan... everything. You're just too good."

Their escapade was bringing out his bad side, which made him mad.

How could he have let her do this to him again? Time after time, he had told himself how to handle it.

Like a fool, he never learned.

"Liss, I've had enough of this. I'm turning around, and going back. I need to shoot up crazy bad, but I don't want to be down here after dark any longer. I'll pay for a taxi to meet us at the bridge to take us into Laredo tonight. We can score there because we have friends, so let's ditch this place now, and fast."

"My grandfather died, so my father took over the ranch," she said softly as she watched him turn back. "He really didn't have a choice, Trevor."

"That's a cop out, and you know it. Everyone has a choice, Liss. Your father could have put the ranch up for sale, instead of moving in. I know folks who would give their eye teeth for a spread like that."

"Two thousand acres on the Rio Grande River? Most of them riverfront? We'd still be waiting for the sale. Think about that, Trev. With your head."

She stared at him as if she had never seen him before, almond eyes traveling down past his chest.

With a coy smile, she pursed her lips and blew him a kiss. At times like these it was hard to believe that they were just friends. Lissy was beautiful in the shadows and danger or not, he was glad to be here. Without another word, she, too, began to turn back.

"Thanks, Liss."

Just then, she heard a grunt in the darkness.

"I think its Raul, hush."

As the silhouette of a man appeared from behind a shack, she shushed him again.

"Let me do the talking," she said under her breath.

"You didn't tell him you were coming alone, did you?" Trevor whispered back.

"Because with a looker like you, Liss, he's probably interested in more than the cash, if you catch what I'm saying. I smell trouble, so get ready to run."

Annoyed, she snorted and tossed her hair back.

He meant it this time, he really did. The short, beady-eyed Mexican now was giving him an evil glare.

"Hush, Trevor, I'll handle this."

After exchanging a few hushed words with the wary man in broken Spanish, she reached for the small sack as he grabbed the wad of cash from her hand.

"My friend Trevor here wants to know if you could also score us some hash- enough for a bowl. Whatever you have, we'll pay you for it."

Another rapid succession of words was exchanged. Lissy, in spite of her poor understanding of the language, was quick to understand.

"He said that he only deals in cocaine, but that he knows where we can get it," she said with a laugh. "We just have to walk a little further down the street, Trev. We'll score your hash and then we'll split. *Entender?* Or shall I say "Do you understand?"

Laughing softly, she glanced at the Mexican.

"How much is this going to cost?" asked Trevor.

He wasn't convinced, and still smelled a rat.

"We don't have that much cash left, Lissy."

If it was some really good stuff, maybe they should go in on it. Maybe, if the price was fair. He loved getting high with her, that was a given. But, his stomach was cramping again. Another round of words was exchanged, most which he couldn't understand.

"Two hundred bucks, Trev," she said, her eyes shining. "It's gold, the best. It'll keep us high for hours. And its right down this road, we just fork over the cash. Come on, we came all this way down here..."

"We live right over there, Liss," he told her, pointing off towards the border. "We can come back down here again."

The man had taken to giving him the evil eye again, one hand to his chest. And he had no idea what was up with that. But, Lissy always knew how to work him, and besides, all the talk about smoking a bowl made him thirsty for it.

"Well, stop talking and get walking. Time's a 'wastin, Liss."

He was surprised to hear himself say that. Every now and then, he could be the comedian. Raul didn't really seem like such a bad cat, it was just his nerves getting the best of him.

Falling into line behind the silent man, they held hands. Now, even if they wanted to, it was too late to turn back. They walked in silence, kicking up dust with their shoes, and neither of them looked behind them. After what seemed like forever, they froze in their footsteps as Raul suddenly halted.

"He says this is it. He wants us to wait here," she said, exchanging words with the Mexican.

With a quick look around him, the man took off in a vapor of dust, the rancid air smelling of dirt, and sweat. They were far from the familiar comfort of the bridge, but they were here.

It was far from a comforting thought, but they *were* finally here.

Trevor let the relief was over him, although it was short lived. They had traveled deeper into Juarez than either of them had planned just to score some meth, but then, crazier things had been negotiated down here. But if this hash was Mexican gold, well, that made all the difference.

He recited a silent prayer, one his mother had taught him as a kid as Lissy started talking to herself again. Her easy-going and childish persona was just one of the reasons that they were such good friends. Taking her hand, he pulled her down into the grass.

Why couldn't she see him as more than a friend? What was it going to take for her to ever listen to him?

As the grass flattened beneath their laughter, the man reappeared from behind a nearby shed as Trevor grabbed Lissy's hand. Without a word, the Mexican placed a small bag into her hand.

"Raul wants us to smoke with him," she said. "He says that he likes crazy Americans, especially those willing to talk to him."

The Mexican's eyes were wild, crazy, as he sat on the grass beside them.

"I told him that it would be alright with you, Trevor. Just a token of peace between borders. *Entender?*

Here, let me light it for you," she said as the Mexican produced a small bowl filled with the hash and placed it before them. "Cluck, cluck, chicken, Trev! Who wants to be the first to suck this baby in?"

As she lit the bowl, he caught his breath. The Mexican seemed nervous, and kept glancing towards the shed.

"What's his problem?" Trevor whispered to Lissy. "Why is he scoping out the shed? If this is a bust, we're so dead."

"Shush…" she hushed him again. "Look, take it easy. We're not under Texas law here. We're south of the border; they do things differently down here."

"That's what worries me," he said, breathing the smoke in.

The hash was good, almost too good, sweet and purer than he had ever smoked before, and clung to his throat like honey as he let it all in, the rush that he lived for flooding over him once again. Yet the Mexican was still making him nervous.

Didn't they kill people for a dollar down here? In fact, he was pretty sure they did.

Taking a long, deep breath, he passed her the bowl so that she could suck it in.

"Inhale it good and deep, baby. Like you said, this stuff's the best."

After the second hit, he wasn't afraid of their shifty new friend, for the Mexican was no longer there. Nor did he have any worries about the abandoned shed, or what was

41

behind it. Whatever the beady-eyed Mexican had given them had made it all worth it- it was that good.

"Liss?"

Miles away, Trevor's eyes glazed over as he stared at Liss, first at her shapely, tanned legs, then at her long, safflower hair. As she sucked up the smoke, she blew it towards him.

"Did someone call my name?" she asked, her eyelids slowly closing. "You need to relax, Trev. Take a tip from Raul here."

The drug dealer was already in a state of complete oblivion, even after just one hit.   No doubt he had been under the influence long before their presence in his land.

Smiling softly at the Mexican, she held out her hand, as he shook his head, refusing her gesture of friendship. The Mexican's strange behavior alarming Trevor, he rolled his eyes at Lissy, and then whispered.

"This guy gives me the creeps. Let's get out of here."

"Lately everyone gives you the creeps, Trevor. Especially me. Get used to it."

Ignoring Trevor and the man, and stretching out on the night grass, she closed her eyes and folded her hands behind her head. Without warning, the Mexican got up, disappearing without a word into the blackness past the shack.

"I tell you, Liss," said Trevor. "Something's not right, I can feel it. Get up, Lissy, now."

It was a warning that he meant every word of, as he pulled her to her feet.

"Let go, you're hurting me, Trev."

"Look, we're getting out of here now. That nutcase just left. Doesn't that tell you something, Liss?"

"That "nutcase," said Lissy, "has the most potent meth that we'll ever smoke or melt down, and, my delusional friend, you are sadly suffering from a severe case of paranoia caused by the lack of it. Look. If you don't have anything good to say, then be silent."

Wobbly on her feet and high from the hash, she took a punch at him and missed. Seizing the opportunity, he grabbed her, pulling her along behind him through the dark in the direction of El Paso and the bridge.

"We're getting out of here, Lissy."

It was no longer a plea or a question, but a command.

"Trevor Joe Mansfield, you let go and you let go now."

"Not until we're out of here. Hold on, I don't want to hear another word from you, Liss."

With a firm hold on her wrist, he pulled her along just as fast as he could, breaking out into a full-on sprint. Past the cardboard shanties and the dirty kids, past the wooden shacks, past a huddle of Mexicans up to who knew what beside one of them. As one of the men turned to watch them pass, a shot rang out from somewhere in the darkness.

"Faster, Lissy," he said, running quickly in the direction of the bridge. "That blast came from somewhere right behind us. Run!"

Holding her tighter, he ran as if their lives depended on it as another shot rocketed past.

"Those bastards are shooting at us. I swear..."

Ducking for cover behind a sheet of plywood, he covered her mouth as he fell on top of her.

"Shush. Don't say anything, Liss."

Somewhere out in the black, the brush crackled, as he listened.

Footsteps? Coming for them?

Struggling to loosen his grip on her, Lissy slapped him, the paranoid behavior just too much for her to handle.

"Trevor Mansfield, this has to end. We came down here for meth, and I want it. If you weren't scared of your own ass, we could have been double dipping back there."

Her almond eyes had become dark with hatred, and he was sad. After several minutes of silence without another shot echoing past, he got up and pulled her to him again.

"Run, Liss. Come on. Get a move on it."

As they ran, he could tell she was tiring, but they were in sight of the cement structure that would carry them over the border. As they flew through the mud down the darkened path, a cat flashed past, disappearing into the grass.

"You got what you wanted; we're at the bridge," said Liss. "And before we cross back into El Paso, I'm melting down some meth. You can be scared if you want, but I choose to shoot up, and I choose to shoot up now, right after we smoke another bowl of hash. You can join me if you want. Are you with me? Or are you afraid, Trev? Because if you are, I'll make you do the chicken dance again."

Like the crazy girl that she was, the girl that was his Liss, she swiveled her hips towards him.

"There's no such thing as the chicken dance," Trevor said.

But the old Liss was back, relieving their stress, and he was glad.

"Oh yes, there is, Trev."

Smiling slyly, she pulled out the small package and sat down in the grass.

"Chick, chick, *chicken*! Sit down, Trevor!"

Tired of arguing with her, he gave in.

Placing a small amount of the hash into the bowl, she placed a match below it, and then breathed in.

"Now *this* is living, Trev. This is why we came down here."

As she passed him the bowl, he sucked it in, the burning substance filling his lungs with that happy feeling again.

"Yeah, it sure is. Maybe I was just being a little too whacked out, Lissy."

High as the air, he lay with his back to a boulder, letting it all sink in.

"You can say that again," Lissy said. "Juarez is fairly safe, Trevor. And besides, we're kids."

"It doesn't matter, Lissy. There are bad people everywhere."

Forgetting everything again, even the bridge, he watched the stars move through the night air.

"How's your stomach?"

As always, he was worried about her.

"Fine now. Yours?"

"Good. After that last hit, that is."

He was at one with the night sky, a star. A star of gold, and diamonds.

"Trev?"

"What, Liss? I'm a shooting star. Watch me shoot away from here."

The hash was overpowering him, but it was good, and he liked it. One eye open, he winked at Liss.

"Shooting star it is then. Let's shoot up some meth."

Like Trevor, although he would never admit it, Lissy was craving something stronger, and craving it bad. Besides, he had almost spoiled everything with his damn paranoia and bolt for the bridge.

"Just once, Trevor, and then we'll head back."

Her gaze was seductive, luring his every breath.

"Aw, Liss..."

Wasting good meth after already feeling the buzz from the hash wasn't exactly his thing, but he didn't really have a problem with it when she looked at him like that.

"I'd rather save it, but you go ahead."

A shooting star, he floated above the bridge, and the night air of the Juarez horizon.

"Chick! Chick! Chick! *Chicken*," she taunted.

Since she obviously wasn't going to take 'no' for an answer, he reluctantly gave in.

"Only upon your solemn promise that we'll head straight home after this. It's late, Lissy. I know I keep telling you this, but it's getting ridiculous that you refuse to listen."

"I wouldn't call 8:00 late, Trev."

"Whatever. Keep a lookout then. And just once, Liss."

"Once it is."

Satisfied, she laid back upon her own rock and patch of grass.

"If you're lucky, maybe you'll reach Pluto or Jupiter, Trev."

"No doubt about that, Liss."

He felt safe now, any danger far past. He had imagined it, like she said. Everything was pure and good now that he was at one with the stars. The meth, Liss, even the rock against his back. Yes, life was good, and it couldn't get much better. Flicking the shoelace at her playfully, he tied it around his upper arm, and prepared to shoot up the meth. The creamy liquid shined bright in the moon-lit air, as he drew it up into the syringe.

With her tell-tale smile, Lissy chewed the tip of a fingernail as she brushed back a stray lock of hair, watching the meth that Raul had given them disappear into Trevor's skin.

This was why the lanky young man who had been born and raised in El Paso was her very best friend. She could always count on him. Anytime, anywhere, he was there.

47

Squeezing his hand playfully, eyes to the stars, she sighed, content. After he passed her the needle, Trevor wasn't going to be the only one flitting around the galaxy somewhere. They'd flit together, arm in arm, exploring one universe to the next. Anxious to inject and join Trevor's party in the stars, she tied the shoelace around her upper arm, and patted his hand.

"Trev? Got your eyes on those planets up there?"

But Trevor didn't answer because he was dead.

Investigation

In the days that followed after Trevor's tragic death, nothing mattered, she didn't expect anything to, or care. Not about cheer practice, or friends, only getting high made her feel halfway alive and human, which she did on a daily basis. Spending another day alone staring out into the field where Trevor used to practice, she cursed Juarez and everything about it, and injected. Just a little at first. Meth that wasn't from Raul's poison stash. Enough to get her past that place which no longer existed. And then a little more, in an effort to get the nightmares to disappear, as she spent more and more time alone with her demons.

She was to blame for his murder, she was sure of it; as she thought about how much that Trevor had adored playing football. It had been his life, and what was going to get him out of El Paso, next to her. The worst part about it was that he hadn't wanted anything to do with Raul; it was she who had coerced him, which made her his murderer. Summer was waning, and it was almost time to return to school, but she didn't care.

As the funeral procession rolled slowly down the street along the Rio Grande River, the procession of vehicles parading past like fallen rockets, her thoughts scattered, like Trevor's ashes. A passenger in Steven's silver pickup, and positioned in line behind Trevor's parents, she sat disengaged at the window, to the right of her mother. As a motorcycle cop drove past, somber face upon her, she buried her head in her hands and broke into tears. Everything made her think of Trevor, especially the cop's helmet. Stomach cramping, she swallowed back the vomit.

The untimely death of the high school's tight end had led to an autopsy and federal investigation, making it no longer possible for her to conceal her addiction. The coroner's report had revealed that Trevor had died from tainted methamphetamine, cocaine laced with substantial traces of bleach and arsenic. As she wept and the small gathering bid farewell to El Paso High's star tight end, the polished brass casket with Trevor's remains was lowered into the earth.

"Have mercy on him, Father," she whispered. "And upon me, for I have sinned."

Placing a rose upon the casket as it descended, she wept.

– – –

The weeks following the funeral were tough, as forensics experts and the F.B.I asked too many questions while drifting through the sprawling home, poking their noses into the most inappropriate places as they questioned her on Trevor's death. Denying any knowledge of anything, and without mention of Raul, she talked candidly about how they had crossed the border on a dare, and how she had accompanied him to go bar hopping in Juarez.

Eyes as calm as the river, as she gazed at the cattle in the pasture, she relayed somberly to the investigators how Trevor had balked at the thought of partying down there alone, and had asked her to come along. With an orchestrated patience, she led them on a well-rehearsed dead end, claiming that by the time she had met up with him in Juarez that he had been in the presence of friends. She explained how the group of kids from their school had left the border city as soon as they had run out of money, and had taken their wallets, leaving them stranded. It was a tough time mentally and physically, as she tried desperately to adjust to Trevor's death and to secure another source for her addiction- one that wouldn't take her upon the streets of Juarez.

She had no alibi, but she didn't care, for she wasn't a suspect in the death because no meth had been found in her system. Only the hash showed loud and clear, as she came clean with her parents, owning up to having smoked it a couple of days prior, and just once, to celebrate the end of her sophomore year.

Her story wasn't perfect, but it was good, good enough to keep the Feds off her tail as they sought an imaginary suspect in Juarez. Down to the last minute detail, she provided the investigators with a graphic and misleading description of a tall, thin man of Mexican-American descent, one who sported a black baseball cap upon one ear, a man by the name of Pablo, and who had dealt them the meth just across the border at Juarez. As the case was postponed, pending new evidence due to Pablo's lack of presence, her hatred for Raul and what he had done to Trevor grew like the weeds that were surrounding the stately ranch home.

Her anger at Trevor's death came in the guise of nightmares- Trevor dead in a desolate field somewhere in Juarez, a knife protruding from his back. Trevor tied naked to a pole like a scarecrow with a bag of meth stuffed into his mouth, then lit on fire, as she raced across the field to save him, but she never made it in time.

Although she was an addict, she had thought things out, and thought them out well before she talked. It's not that she didn't want Raul hunted down and sentenced for Trevor's death, she did, but testifying against him in court was a different matter. Reprisal from the cartels in Juarez or anywhere across the globe was a realistic danger, and while she wanted justice for Trevor's death, the reality was that she couldn't really do anything about it. In a perfect world, one in which the high-powered cartels didn't exist, she could have the murderous bandit taken out on the street by hiring someone to do it for her- a paid assassin. But it wasn't a perfect world, and justice wouldn't be served in the manner that she might have liked it. Besides, people were murdered every day, and not just by the Mexican cartels. Things happened.

What good would life in prison do her, anyway? That was no way to pay homage to Trevor.

As she walked across the football field, she went crazy thinking about it.

An accident. Just like the 'accident' that had happened to Trevor. In a perfect world that didn't exist- anywhere. Some of her friends' parents had money, or she could ask her father. She had to be losing her mind, or quite possibly she had already lost it.

She pictured Trevor playing football, rehearsing excuses to tell her father.

The tall, lanky frame and squared shoulders, the tousled auburn, sun-kissed hair and that enduring smile... the way that he blocked a pass and darted down the field-

It was the little things that mattered, and that she would remember.

The wide, grassy field, somber after a day of practice; the sophomore hall where she had been assigned a locker.

Her first day as a freshman, before afternoon history class, when she had been having trouble opening her locker- it had been Trevor who had been there to help her. Appearing slyly from behind a corner of the corridor- he had flipped the lock around in a frenzy that had made her dizzy and, presto! It was open.

Nothing that was anything would ever be the same without him- ever. Not homeroom where they aimed spit wads at the ceiling as Professor Thornton lectured; unaware of what was transpiring behind him. Not Friday night football games or practice, or getting high and driving without a license. Sitting in the empty field, she started crying, remembering how Trevor had been looking forward to another season of practice. He had gone so far as to demand that she attend each and every one of his games, and she had nodded her agreement with a smile.

He was in his glory in this field, and now he was dead. Murdered by some Mexican bandit under the thumb of some drug lord in Juarez.

In spite of the circumstances of his death, she vowed to remember the good things, like how he laughed, and how he would always eat a huge plate of spaghetti right before every practice. That's what she would remember. Not the way that he his lip had curled up from the poison that had killed him, but the light of his face when she had been with him, and in the field, forever.

As he called her name from out across the grass, she reached for the needle. It was nearing dusk and she was in shorts, the metal bleacher pressing coldly against her flesh, but her thoughts were colder. Within seconds of shooting up the meth, she was a freshman again, and back to happier times with her best friend. As he reached for a pass, she shot up again.

--- --- ---

Maybe that's why the investigators had returned. The recurring nightmares, her reclusive behavior, the flashbacks of Trevor's mouth stuffed with meth.

Or the fact that her parents had discovered a needle.

Like a lone soldier, it had announced its presence beneath her bed in a flash of silver, shining its boldness upon the faces of her distraught parents.

Like any other intelligent, adolescent girl, she had vehemently denied it at first, just like she had denied any knowledge of their wrongdoings in Juarez the month prior. Yet although young and bright, she was first and foremost an addict, hopelessly addicted and incapable of covering her tracks because she just couldn't remember. With the discovery of the needle, and of the lone shoelace that was confiscated from the tiled floor of the lavatory, the Feds had closed in, prodding and poking and asking too many questions, and although she had denied its existence, they didn't listen, but insisted on testing her.

"The results of your daughter's tests were positive," someone in a cold, dark suit had relayed to her parents.

Oh, how she had shamed them! And how sorry she was for it, but so unable to do anything about it.

"With the existence of this new evidence, we're holding your daughter pending bail, Mr. Boming," he had finished with.

"My daughter isn't a criminal," Steven had answered. She's never been arrested. This is an outrage. May I ask, under what charge?"

His argument being quickly washed down the toilet, Steven had hung his head, defeated and dejected. As he wiped a stray hair from his face, Lissy had seen the tears.

"Under the influence of an illegal substance, that said substance being cocaine."

The agent's tone was flat, dull, and without air, after which he firmly twisted the shackles around Lissy's wrists.

"The maximum amount of time that we can hold her pending trial is seventy two hours, sir."

Meant to soothe, the statement missed its mark.

"Pending trial?" Steven asked. "For what? "I'm afraid that isn't going to happen."

"Sir, "the agent said, "Being under the influence of an illegal substance carries criminal penalties under the law, and is a crime that we can charge your daughter for. Look, she isn't the only kid with a problem. Take a look around you. Have you forgotten that you live in El Paso? Drug use is a growing epidemic here."

What Steven noticed next was that the man in the suit who had just cuffed his only daughter was smiling. Because of that smile, the very next day, a sign was erected in the grass at the ranch house.

"Daddy," Lissy said, wrestling with the handcuffs. "I didn't mean to hurt you, I'm sorry. Don't waste your money on posting bail; I'll be out in a matter of hours."

She would be out in hours, so what was the point of paying to get out? Nothing.

"I won't have my daughter in jail, not one..."

Before Steven could finish speaking, Lissy stopped him.

"Daddy, look. It's only seventy two hours. Come on. I can handle it."

Always one to get her way, she wouldn't take no for an answer, watching in anger as the two men confiscated the rest of her stash- a glass pipe, a lighter, and a bowl, for evidence. What made it worse was the smile on both of their faces.

"It's only three days," she said again, ignoring the men. "I'll be home before you know it."

It wasn't the 72 hours that had her bothered, but the fact that she would be without any meth for the duration of her stay there. Sometimes, it was possible to score behind the iron doors, in which case she could avoid being dope sick and suffering from acute withdrawals.

"Don't worry," she said to Steven as she was ushered off toward the patrol car. "It's Trevor that needs your prayers, Daddy, so that Jesus will let him into Heaven."

As she climbed into the rear seat behind the glass panel, Lissy saw that Steven was crying.

As the car pulled away from the driveway, Lissy gazed sadly at the expansive ranchland and pastures, waving goodbye to Marie and Steven from behind the panel, terrified about withdrawing from cocaine and being dope sick in jail. There was nothing worse than being dope sick in the entire world. Nothing. It was the worst possible feeling imaginable.

Picture the worst flu known to man. It was much worse than that.

She would be nauseous, her limbs would spasm, they would have a hard time holding her down, and then the convulsions would follow. And that was just the beginning.

As she contemplated being violently ill in a cement cell with no medications provided, not even an aspirin, she watched the fence posts fly by and the cattle chew the grass as they foraged for flowers. Contrary to what most city folk believed to be true, cattle, and especially longhorn cattle, were highly intelligent. She watched quietly as the sturdy necks bobbed up, then down, in their quest for the flowers which grew wild in the fields. She adored the cattle, especially the calves that were born each summer.

As the patrol car sped along towards the highway, she watched the whitewashed lettering on the For Sale sign fade behind her.

Alta

As the patrol car drove silently along the river, she stared blankly through the bulletproof panel at the rippling waters of the Rio Grande. Although her last fix had only been four or five hours ago, she was already suffering acute withdrawals. They drove first to the station, where she was charged with a single count of being under the influence of an illegal substance, and a secondary charge of paraphernalia possession. She was now on her way to the coed county holding facility of Alta, a thirty minute drive from El Paso. She was fortunate to be a first time offender, as Brisley, the federal prison for women in Central Texas, housed women convicted of violent crimes in the same holding tank and cell blocks as minor offenders. As the river narrowed and the scrub oak turned to concrete, she clutched at her cramping stomach and knocked her head against the panel in anguish.

Although she was confined to the rear seat of the patrol car, there was something comforting about the muddy river, a 2,000 mile span of winding and meandering water which spanned the land from Colorado to Mexico. Christened "Big River," by the colonial Spanish, it emitted a murky odor in the heat of summer, algae present in its depleted stream. In northern Colorado, its treacherous banks flanked by tall pines, it meandered lazily along through the international border crossing of Ciudad, Juarez, the scrub oak of the desert giving way to deep cuts in the banks due to the felling of pines. By the time it had flowed past the spacious ranch in El Paso, it had emptied its bed load and run out of steam. In the early evenings, after the dinner dishes had been washed and put away, she could count on the company of mule deer and antelope, along with the occasional jackal. As she watched it fade behind her, she was filled with apprehension and sadness.

The pains that had come these last few weeks were strong and frightening, pains that emerged from the deepest recesses of her stomach, worse than any flu that she had ever suffered or could imagine. Far worse than when she had been casually using, now the only way to make the pain stop was to shoot up again in the cycle of addiction, until she was a full-fledged addict with a minimum of a thrice-daily habit. Now, hit with another knife-like pain, and doubled over, she clenched her stomach, panicking over her zero chance to get any meth into her system. As the patrol car drove leisurely in the direction of Alta, she quietly suffered.

From past experience, she knew that next would come the bouts of vomiting and diarrhea, along with a rapid pulse and high fever, and then, when she was ready to end it all; the uncontrollable spasms that threatened to send her through the ceiling. As another pain ripped through her middle and she doubled over again in spasm, she tried desperately to get her mind of her problems by watching the river.

The last rays of day upon the darkening skyline, she thought about her charges that were criminal in nature. In her life, she had never even ridden in a police car, much less confined to the rear seat of one like a common criminal. But then, that was before the two counts against her- the felony charge of being under the influence and the misdemeanor of paraphernalia possession. The only "good" thing about going to Alta was that after she had served her 72 hours, she had the opportunity to enter a rehab facility for 90 days so that the felony charge wasn't on her record.

As the light left the horizon for good, giving way to a lavender sky, the patrol car rolled methodically down the long drive towards the tall, secure facility that was Alta. Stark and oppressive, the ancient, brick building stood solemn in the distance. As the fear rose in her stomach, Lissy vomited on the floorboard.

"End of the road. Out," a gruff voice demanded as the vehicle rolled to a stop at the end of the drive. "That means you, girlie."

Doubled over in pain, she obeyed, but only after spewing more vomit. Her pale pink blouse splattered in vomit, she heard the sound of laughter.

"Well, hot dawg! Another addict!" the guard said in a pelt of laughter. "You'll have to be tougher than that, sister, or da ladies here will beat da living daylights out of yo. Da vomit, too, that matter. Yo best get it out of yo system now and puke another time o two before we reach da entrance."

Grabbing Lissy's handcuffs, she dragged her along, motioning at the dirt to the side of the drive as Lissy moaned in agony.

"I can't do this. You can't make me. I'm sick," Lissy protested.

Yet, doing as ordered, she spewed vomit until her throat burned.

"Please... ma'am. I can't help it, I'm an addict."

"Sister," the guard said, eyeing her warily. "We're all addicts; every jailbird here is an addict, so no matter how much yo vomit, yo won't get special treatment. So- puke out yo guts and get over it."

On command, Lissy lurched over, vomiting until the liquid ran clear and she was dizzy with exhaustion.

"Now, sister, that's mo like it!"

Looking at Lissy like she might do tricks or put a spell on her, the guard grabbed her handcuffs again and pushed her back into the police car, then drove in the direction of the iron gates of Alta.

"Look, it's not that I'm trying to disobey, but I just can't do this, I'm sick," Lissy said again, as if it mattered. "I need medical detox, not jail time. I'm not a criminal, I'm an addict."

This elicited another enormous round of laughter as the guard ushered Lissy inside the jail.

"Girlfriend, like I done told yo, everyone here's an addict, so get over it," the guard repeated, marching Lissy through a trio of thick double doors before shackling her to a group of prisoners. Attired in standard orange jumpsuits and paper slippers, the female inmates were rude and wary.

"And if yo smart, yo get over it- sooner than later."

With this, the guard departed, leaving her shackled and in the presence of another female guard, who saluted Lissy disrespectfully. As the inmates laughed at her, Lissy vomited.

"Girl, that ain't no way to get yo groove on," someone beside her snickered. "That's not how we treat our sisters."

Afraid to answer, lest she vomit, Lissy hung her head in silence.

She was sick, real sick, and much too sick to deal with any of these foolish idiots, and if she didn't get medical attention right away, well, she couldn't be held responsible for what might happen. Trying to lift her head, she vomited.

"Girl, yo trippin'?" someone said through the laughter. "Can't do no trippin' here.

Lissy looked up to see her fellow 'sister,' an inmate with yellow nails and bobbed, flame-orange hair.

"Look, sister," the inmate said. "If yo need to puke, point it at the corner."

As more laughter rang out, Lissy vomited. Her stomach depleted even of vomit, she fell exhausted to the cement in a fetal position.

"Just another addict," the inmate said, mimicking the departed guard. "So girlfriend, how does it feel to be just another addict, like the rest of us?"

As Lissy laid dope sick and silent on the cold cement, the woman coughed long and raspy into her shackles.

"Welcome to Alta," in a round of laughter, was all she heard before passing out in the corridor.

She woke to the shrill ring of a bell, the kind that was used at dark to herd cattle back into their corrals, in a small, narrow cell harshly lit with a single bulb that smelled of dirty laundry. Raising her head slowly off the metal cot, she ventured a look around her. The bright, white lighting made it hard to see, as she tried to focus. The only furniture in her 'room' was an empty cot and a single toilet without a lid in the corner. Upon the realization that she was alone, she wept, exhausted. Lying back down upon the metal, she contemplated her sorry situation.

She remembered little about what had transpired before, other than hitting her head upon the unforgiving floor and vomiting her guts out several times over. As another bout of queasiness came over her, the bars to her cell shook boldly as a muscular female entered. Lifting her head from the cot, she saw the procession of shackled prisoners.

"Up, yo," the guard said as she shackled Lissy to them. "Time's a wastin.'"

"Single file, no running, move slowly, or I'll use this on yo all," the guard said, waving a club into the line of prisoners.

Whereas Lissy had been hoping for a drink of water, or something to settle her stomach, what she got was a shocking introduction to the intake procedures of female prisoners. Shuffling through the hall as it wound through the corridors, she marched methodically with the others into a cold, concrete room with communal showers. To her horror, she was forced to disrobe and step naked beneath them.

"Three minutes, sister, so get to it!" a harsh voice demanded as a whistle was blown.

"Here yo soap and brush."

Lissy took the items offered and stepped beneath the shower. With a mournful squeak, the spigot turned on, showering her with icy water. Sixty seconds later, a rough, cloth towel was thrown at her. There had been no time to lather up with the soap, much less to use it.

"Time's UP!" The voice demanded. "Yo all be yo doggies NOW!"

Just when she thought that things couldn't get any worse, she was forced to the concrete floor, as a pair of gloved hands worked her over.

"All clean here!" A shrill voice piped as the gloves raked through her hair. The way they tore into her reminded her of sandpaper.

"Crevices clean and accounted for!" the voice said.

Lissy wasn't sure what was worse- coming down off the meth, or having her lips pulled in all directions as the thick glove forced itself in.

"Thirty seconds!" the voice demanded, tossing Lissy the orange jumpsuit. "That means you, Blondie!"

Eyes on the floor and unable to help herself, Lissy vomited on the jumpsuit.

"This ain't no coffee break! Up to it!" the guard said, grabbing her hair and shackling her back to the prisoners.

Handicapped by the oversize jumpsuit and slippers, Lissy stumbled with the other inmates back to her cell, the heavy bars locking into place behind her.

"That's yo first write up, Blondie," the guard accused, glaring while smacking her lips, gum sticking out between them. "Two more and yo lose yo privilege to shower. If I can make a suggestion, splash yo ass faster tomorrow."

With another smack of the lips, high on rudeness, she disappeared down the hallway, leaving Lissy alone in the harsh light of her confinement.

She had absolutely no idea what a 'write up' was, or how much time had passed since her admission to Alta, for it was impossible to decipher day from night beneath the constant glare of the overhead. Tears wetting the thin jumpsuit, she laid down upon the metal bed, listening to the misery around her.

Much worse than not knowing whether it was day or night, was hearing the heartache in the stale air, the inmates moaning in dope sick agony, screaming and beating their heads against the walls in the harshness of the lighting. A howl echoed from down the hall, a 'sister' in the thralls of a mental breakdown.

"Get me out! Help me!" She shrieked.

Yet no one lent an ear.

"This is torture! This is hell! I don't belong in this shithole! Get me out!"

The pitiful cries for help made Lissy cringe, as she hid her head in her hands while trying to stay warm beneath the thin sheet provided.

"None of us belong in here you raving lunatic!" A voice thundered from somewhere in the whiteness. "Shut your trap or I'll shut it for you!"

Lissy prayed as the woman's screams echoed another decibel louder.

Just two more days. 48 hours. I only have to get through 48 more hours.

I can handle it. I can do it. God help me.

The woman's pain had almost made her forget her own pathetic misery, as her stomach lurched and the cramping grew stronger. When the headache came on above her right temple, she cried out, unable to help it. Spasms in her legs doubled her over as the screams down the corridor growing louder.

"Stop your howling! I'm having a panic attack and can't breathe!" Lissy screamed.

Attempting to silence the crazed woman, she pounded at the relentless bars, spraining her hand before collapsing in a corner.

"We all want out! Are you an idiot?"

Screaming had made her throat hurt, and she was desperate for some meth and a glass of water. She had told her father that she could handle this, but now she wasn't so sure.

"Someone help me! Please!" she screamed into the air.

She could raise her voice all she wanted, but no one was there to listen.

"I'm dope sick and I can't be here!" she screamed again. "You've got to give me something for it! I'll die if I don't get some help immediately, and a glass of water!"

The more that she voiced her objections, the louder that the voice down the hall became.

Someone within the miserable facility was going to have to listen to her, or she would die here.

What was with the Texas law of not being able to post bail for 72 hours? That was the most ridiculous thing that she had ever heard. What an asinine state! She was hating it more each day.

Suddenly, a paper sack was shoved through an opening below the bars. Curious, she tore it open.

Not even a stinking cup of water!

In the sack was a carton of tepid milk, an apple, and a piece of bologna with four slices of cheap bread. She was allergic to milk, and had been since she was a baby. She tried to eat the bologna between two slices of bread, and vomited.

"I'm allergic to milk! Please, someone help me! I need water!"

Not a guard in the narrow hallway, her cries met only silence.

She was going to die in this hellhole, she just knew it.

How long could someone live without water? And what if they were dehydrated from vomiting?

Sicker than she had ever been, she forced herself to eat between bouts of vomiting up her stomach contents. To keep her legs from jumping up into the air, she laid in a fetal position upon the metal bed, and held them to her stomach, continuing her plea for water. As she lay shaking, in danger of suffering a convulsion, she heard a voice from the next cell over.

"Girl, some sisters have been in this stinkpot for a year, and you'll be out of here in hours. I'd give anything to be in you. You need to give your thanks, sister."

What was this? What planet were these women on?

"A year? For what?" Lissy said.

"You know, the usual," the woman continued through the cement. "Being under the influence, possession. And sometimes that's only for a second offense. But it don't matter what you're here for at Alta. Unless you're in protective custody, everyone's treated the same."

Protective custody? What was that?

The conversation with the inmate was taking her mind off of how sick she was.

"Protective custody?" Lissy asked. "What's that?"

"Girlfriend," the inmate said. "You mean to tell me that you haven't heard of protective custody? We call it "PC" here. Protective custody is for those folks who are in here for messing around with kids. Perverts, sister. Sexual predators."

"Oh," Lissy said. "Yeah, I get it."

"Look, this is how it is," the woman continued. "If they let them out in the general population, we'd kill their asses. Protective custody. From the rest of us. That's why they're dressed in red. Say, what are you in for, sister?"

"Under the influence and possession of paraphernalia," Lissy answered, feeling a little better and sitting in the corner. "I'm here for the 72 hours until my parents are allowed to post bail. I wasn't booked for dealing or anything, just being under the influence. Things have been pretty rough for me lately. My best friend was killed while we were down trying to score in Juarez."

"I'm sorry to hear," the inmate said. "I bet you've learned your lesson about going down there."

"Yeah, I guess," Lissy answered.

"Well, sister, you're lucky," the woman continued as Lissy listened. "If they had gotten you for possession and you had already flunked out of Prop, they'd give you a year. Minimum. That's Texas law for you. It sucks. Bad."

"Prop? What's that?" Lissy said.

She didn't really want to talk to anyone in here, but she'd be out in a matter of hours. Like the woman said, she was lucky. Lissy just had to keep remembering that.

"Proposition 36, you know- the drug treatment program. The one for first time offenders. Come on, sister, get with it. This is how it goes down here. First, they get you for possession; next, they send your ass to the program, then IF you're lucky, you don't mess up again, and that's the end of it. I can't believe you haven't heard of the program."

"Well, I haven't," Lissy said. "Should I have? Sorry."

Now she was sorry that she had ever started talking to the woman, because she just kept on going, and going, and going.

"The program is really just a mandatory class," the inmate continued as Lissy held her legs to keep them from shaking.

"You start out by testing once a week, and if you test 'dirty' or 'positive' they up it. And if you keep testing dirty, like almost everyone does, then you wind up here in Alta."

The woman that Lissy couldn't see was one of the resident 'experts,' no doubt. An expert who might know where to get her hands on some meth.

"Hey," Lissy said, her voice shaking. "I need some meth. Do you know where I can get some?"

Her question made the woman laugh.

"Meth, sister? In this joint? Not a chance. But I can hook you up with some downers. Sister goes by the name of "Letty," and deals at the showers. You'll have to be quick, though. And swallow it fast, no questions. Can you handle that?"

"Yes," Lissy whispered. "I can handle it. I don't care what it is, I just want it. Whatever she has."

Desperate for a fix, she would take whatever was available.

"No one will see, I promise," Lissy said.

"Then you've got yourself a deal," the voice said. "You can't wait 72 hours to get your fix? You got it bad, sister."

"I guess," Lissy said.

"Look, ain't no guessing about it. You got it bad, and that's just the way it is. But here's the bad part. You get caught, you don't snitch. No matter what. Ever. Because if you do, you'll be wearing a wristband that shows your true color. 'Blue,' for "I snitched on my sisters." You should see what those poor bastards look like after a week or two and the sisters get hold of them. You can barely recognize them."

"That's not going to happen." Lissy said, thinking about all of the bodies that were dumped beneath the bridge in Juarez. "I would never rat. Especially on a sister."

"Good. You got it," the woman said, banging something against the cement so loud that Lissy's head hurt. "It won't be pretty if you do."

"I got it," Lissy answered. "Letty. Tomorrow. At the showers. Look, I don't feel good, can I talk to you later?"

"Sister, then it's time to throw up your guts again," the woman snickered. "Ain't anything else you can do here. There's nothing that will cure a good dope sick like a good upchuck, then you'll be fresh and rested for tomorrow."

With this final outburst, the woman was silent.

Alone again, Lissy vomited.

"Just throw my guts up," she whispered to the air. "That'll solve it."

Sticking a finger down her throat, she spewed out the bologna and the bread, as another paper sack was shoved beneath the bars.

"Didn't you hear me?" Lissy shouted at the guard. "I'm allergic to milk! I need water!"

"Everyone here is sick, so get used to it," the woman said, staring at Lissy like she was an alien. You eat, you drink, you make your bed, and all before 4 a.m. And I'll tell you once, but not again. When you hear the bell ring, you'll have exactly 30 seconds to line up for the showers. If you're still asleep, or not standing, you'll receive a write-up again. Three of those get you solitaire."

"Of course," Lissy said. "I get it."

She opened the sack to see the standard milk carton and a package of plain instant oats along with a minuscule package of syrup.

Syrup? On oatmeal? And milk? When she was allergic to it?

Now she felt like vomiting again.

"I'm allergic to milk." She whispered again.

"Milk is all you get," the guard said. "Didn't they teach you anything in kindergarten? It has water in it. You need to suck it up; you're being released in twenty four hours."

As the warden disappeared into the stark whiteness of the corridor, Lissy choked down the oatmeal and syrup.

When she tried to rest, the fever began, and in her delusions Trevor appeared, naked and tied to the pole, on fire, just like before, only this time, he was calling out to her as he burned. Over and over again his screams pierced the air as the flames rose around him.

"Trevor, I'm coming!" she said.

And then she bounded towards him, across a mighty field and river, as the flames began licking his chest. No longer was his mouth stuffed with meth, but with a stick of dynamite.

"Trevor! You hold on there! I'm got water!" she shouted as she ran atop the river.

As she watched, his chest melted and the flames rose to light the dynamite, the fuse only inches from his face. She dragged the bucket as she ran, calling out to him.

"Trevor! Hold on, baby! I'm almost there!"

As the dynamite exploded and his face burst, she heard laughter, awakening to a warden standing over her.

"I knew that yo couldn't do it," the guard said. "That's yo second write up, sister. Didn't yo hear? It's 4 a.m. Yo just march yoself over to the end of the line now, single file."

Disoriented, Lissy struggled out of the bed, vomit from the jumpsuit clinging to her wet skin. She wasn't surprised that the nightmares had returned. She knew they would. She just hadn't known when.

Not caring about being 'written up,' because she was being discharged in a matter of hours, Lissy shuffled into line behind the other inmates, as the shackles were attached to her wrists with a pull to her hair.

"Ouch! That hurt!" she said.

Just because she was stuck in jail didn't give them reason to mistreat her.

Or did it?

Instead of an apology, she received a knee to her rear.

"Say 'ouch' again and I won't just pull it, I'll twist it out of yo head," the warden said, shoving her roughly through the corridor. "You're wearing out yo welcome with me here."

As she was shuffled through the cold corridor past cellblocks of chortling inmates, Lissy remembered Letty and her 'stash.'

Could she pull it off? What would happen to her if she didn't?

Falling to her knees from another knife-like pain to her stomach, the warden kicked her again.

The worst that could happen would be more time in jail. She was really sick. She had to risk it.

As the procession reached the showers, she was unshackled, as she removed her jumpsuit to stand naked beneath them.

"Hey, Blondie!" someone shouted. "When we get out of here, can I do ya?"

Ignoring the insult, Lissy showered, the dozen naked women around her drip-drying upon the cement. Just when

76

time was up and the warden blew the whistle, she saw the hulking form in the corner about 10 meters over.

"Letty?" mouthed Lissy as the inmate nodded.

With just seconds to score, Lissy fell to the floor, crying and clutching her stomach as the woman walked towards her.

"Look, we don't have no crybabies here," Letty said, as she kicked her.

With the kick, Letty punched her chest, delivering the narcotic to Lissy's waiting mouth with a quick twist of the wrist.

"Next time I won't be so nice," Letty said, as she walked away from her.

Swallowing quickly, Lissy dissolved any remaining traces of the narcotic with saliva as she coughed to divert attention. With a yank to her hair, the warden pulled her up from the cement.

"This ain't no tea party, Blondie!" she said, pushing her towards inspection of crevices. "That's yo third write-up, so after yo splash yoself, its solitaire."

The warden's voice was gruff and vicious, but Lissy couldn't have cared. The narcotic was taking effect, and she was floating above all the cares and bullshit of the women's prison. If it was confinement they wanted, they were welcome to it, because she was out of her anyway.

Strange, wasn't it, how justice was served? You get a little high in you, and then you don't care?

Lissy hobbled towards the inspection area with a smile, guards surrounding her. She might have another 'write up', but if she could pass the glove test, she was home free, and that was all that mattered.

"# 6297 crevices clean and accounted for!" the warden said with a final finger to her rear. "Move on, missy!"

She had passed the inspection of the rubber fingers with flying colors, all traces of the narcotic nonexistent.

Taking her place in line, and flying high, she was shackled at the wrists and marched humbly down the corridor, as she thought about how good it would feel when she was finally free of her confinement. Whatever 'Letty' had given her, she was grateful for it, and blissful in her euphoria.

"Wet ass coming past!" a guard shouted, a frenzy of chortling in the cells around them.

"#6297- solitaire!"

So- she had been reduced to a number. So what?

As the shackles were yanked from her wrists and the metal door of the solitary cell slammed behind her, she flew high in her euphoria. In the cell, Trevor appeared, his limbs sprouting talons the color of seaweed and the air. He was singing something to her, something she couldn't understand, and could barely hear. As her sang, the chortling began although there were no cells around her, as the ghostly apparition of the sophomore tight end floated through the cement and disappeared.

There was no metal bed in this stateroom, no neighbor to pass the time with. With a final thud of the iron bars, she was left alone in darkness, no bulb above her to shine harshly down upon her. So stupefied was she, so far removed from it all and under the influence of whatever Letty had given her, that she slept for the first time there.

Thirty minutes before the sun rose, she was unshackled, and after a search of her cell and of her body, the jumpsuit was stripped off and her possessions were returned to her, minus her money, after which she was led outside the oppressive gates, the humiliating experience behind her. Her cell phone dead, and without a charger, Lissy took one final glance at the formidable structure before turning in the direction of the Rio Grande.

August 19th, Monday.

My dearest Lissy,

The first and most important thing that I need to tell you is that I love you, and that I miss you so much. More than anything in the world. Today is the third day since you went missing from Alta and haven't come home, but your father and I know that you'll be home soon.

It's important for me to tell you that I have never done this before- written a letter to you, so I'm not really sure where to begin. I've actually started to try to write this letter four times, and I still can't seem to get it right, and find myself staring over and over again at what I write. You know how whenever I have something important to say that I always have to think about it for awhile before I say it? Well, I think that's true for most children and parents, and I think that writing a letter is sort of the same. And then I ask myself "what is right?" and "why can't I get it right?" and the answer that I keep coming up with is that there is no 'right,' way to write, no 'right' thing to say, there's just this incredible love that I have for you, love so powerful and strong that it grows by the day, love that I need to write about now because instead of telling you to your face- kissing you, holding you tight and giving you lots of hugs, I must put on the page until you come home.

You probably don't remember, well, I'm sure that you don't because you were too young, but on the day you were born, your father and I held you in our arms for the entire day just because we could, and because you were so precious and

80

beautiful and because we just didn't want them to take you away from us. So in a way, I think that writing you this letter this is sort of like that, because right now you're away, and because there are things that I want to tell you and say, hugs and kisses I want to give you, but which have to stay on paper for now. I'm not sure if any of this will make sense to you, or if you'll even care, but I'm sure that it will at least be good for a couple of laughs when you get home!

I can't wait for you to come home! I'm going to give you a great, big hug and I'm going to try not to cry, because I know how you hate it when I cry.

I don't know if I should tell you this, because it might make you angry that we resorted to this, but your father and I went down to the police station the night that you didn't' come home so that we could file a missing persons report on you. I think it was the only day of my life that I've been thankful that you're 16, because it meant that we didn't have to wait, and could file the report right away. If you were 18, we would have had to wait for 72 hours before we could report you missing. Since we filed the report, we've been back to the station probably 6 or 7 times to make sure that they're doing everything they can to find you.   It's just so hard to sit and wait, and it's the only thing we seem to be able to do, along with worrying, which doesn't help anything.

The waiting is so frustrating! It's so hard, Lissy!

We can only hope and pray that they're doing everything in their power to find you, which is why we made the decision to place our trust in them, and our faith, in their ability to bring you home. But that doesn't stop me from worrying that, because of your addiction, they might not give your case the same priority that they give to other missing children, because not only did they list you as being an addict, but a runaway, too.

Can you believe that, Lissy! A runaway!?

Your father and I confronted them right then and there, because we know that you never would run away, but they told us that it was procedure, and that there was nothing they could do about it but they had to do it that way, and that you were expected home that afternoon after your release and since there was no reason to suspect foul play, that you were indeed, a 'runaway.'

So tell me, Lissy, because you're always so good at helping me with these things- how can I stop worrying that they might try to locate the children who they truly believe have 'gone missing?' It's in the back of my mind all the time, no matter what I do, no matter what I think. I miss your input on these things!

And then your father and I tried to explain how you have gone missing, and how you would never have run away, and how you have never done anything like this before, and they tell us that there's always a first time for everything, and then it's back to the beginning all over again, where we come home for a little while only to go back there again.

What it comes down to, my precious daughter, is that your father and I can't stop worrying about how you were released from jail three days ago and still haven't contacted us. There could be so many reasons that you haven't picked up the phone, some that I refuse to think about, and it makes me incredibly fearful and sad. You wouldn't understand, but your father and I have to worry, we can't help it because it's in our parental blood because we just don't know where you are.

In saying this, I know how frustrated that you become and how you don't like it when I worry like this, but I just can't seem to stop, it's just the way that your father and I, and all parents, are. One day, if you ever get married and have children of your own, you'll understand. That first afternoon that your firstborn is just ten minutes late walking in that door from school- well, I don't want to scare you, but it's all downhill from there. You start wondering why they're late, and it just goes on from there. And then suddenly, they're there, and it's all okay again, because they're home. Although we don't like it, we can't help ourselves, the nature of worrying is a natural thing that parents do when it comes to their kids. And it's something that's always there, like the love that your father and I have for you. I wish I could keep these awful thoughts from coming, but it's hard, so they keep on running through my head no matter how much I try to stop them. So I get up, stop what I'm doing, drink a glass of water, and then just like every other time, I tell myself not to worry all over again, that at any time you'll come walking in.

Your father called the jail's intake coordinator when you neglected to meet him at the gate to see if they had a security camera at the entrance and to ask if maybe he had your release date wrong, but he was told that the information they had on file was correct, and that you had been released on the day we had been told. So we're thinking that maybe he arrived at the gate too early, or maybe he arrived there too late, and not that the details matter, but your father waited *for hours for you and he tried to call you several times too, but you didn't pick up your phone. And then it started getting dark and he started freaking out (you know how he does!) and then he drove down the road in each direction until he couldn't see anymore, but he still couldn't find you. I can't begin to describe the look on his face when he came in the door that night he was supposed to bring you home. It will stay with me forever, Lissy, no matter how much I don't want it to. You're probably wondering why I am telling you any of this, and what difference any of it makes, so let me see if I can try to explain.*

We love our little girl and we miss her so very much. And your father and I believe that you are alive and well, and will be coming home.

We don't know why you haven't called, but yesterday we found your charger in your desk, so we know that you didn't bring it along. We know how upset you are over Trevor's death, which is why we are keeping to our belief that you just need a few days alone. We trust that you are with friends and that you weren't picked up by someone you didn't know. You have always been such a careful girl about where you go and with whom, at least up until you went with Trevor to Juarez, but we believe that because of Trevor's death that you will never go down there again. Now, when we try to call your cell, it just goes straight to voice mail, which I like to believe is a good thing, because it could mean that you just need to charge your phone. We can't leave any more messages for you, because we've left too many and your mailbox is full. And we don't know why you haven't checked them and called, but it could be because for whatever reason that you weren't given your phone upon release, or it could be

*that you lost it or misplaced it, and please don't get mad at me
for saying this, but it could be that you sold it for drugs.
Whatever the reason is, and why you haven't phoned, we
don't care and we're not going to yell, we just want you home.
And the reason is simple, Liss. You're our only daughter, our
only child and the only thing that matters to us in the world is
our love for you. We miss you so very much.*

*Lissy, please come home, and please come home soon.
We won't ask you any questions, we promise.*

*A lot of thoughts keep running through my mind, many
that I can't or don't want to ask you, and I want you to know
that I know that you didn't ask to be addicted, and if you're
out on another 'high,' that you can still come home. Your
father and I know that when you do come down, instead of
picking up the phone to call us you'll probably decide to get
high again, because not only will you want to, but you'll have
to. It's just what addiction does to you. So, yes, your father
and I know a few things. But it isn't my intent to preach, Lissy,
because you don't need that in your life, we know that the
past couple of years haven't been easy on you and that we put
you through a lot of hard times with the move, and I'm sure
that the first thing you're going to ask me when you come
home is why any of this is important for you to know. Well,
here goes.*

*Because I love you and miss you and because when you
walk through the door, no matter where you've been or why,
you'll know that your father and I love you more than anything
in the world. And because we want you to know that is was a
mistake to move you away from your friends in Austin, and we
take full responsibility for that, because it was your home. If*

we had it to do over again, Lissy, we would never have moved. So yes, I feel that's important for you to know. And then, after we hug and kiss and cry, I can show you this little letter that might not mean much to you, but that I saved for you and that might be a little 'mushy' and stuff, and whether we laugh or cry won't matter, but what will matter is that we're reading it together, you and I. I hope you come home soon, because I miss having you here with me to talk with and laugh with, I miss driving you to school in the morning and home from it, too, you know, the important stuff. Last night at our weekly family dinner, the one that you and I started a few months ago because you were super tired of your father and I bothering you, and because I finally accepted that you're not just older now, but that on weekend nights you want to spend time with friends for awhile, well, Lissy, I really missed you. Your father just came in and said to tell you that he loves you too, with all his heart, and that he can't wait for you to come home.

Yesterday I planted some of those flowers you like, the morning glories, and I hope you like lavender as much as you like blue. They were out of the blue seeds at the store, and the lavender ones looked really pretty. And then because I wasn't paying attention to what I was doing and because I had started worrying again, I poked my finger with the hoe. Just a little bit, I mean it's okay; it won't need stitches or anything like that. Actually, I don't even know why I'm telling you this except that it would never have happened if I didn't miss you so much. Oh, and I saw Trevor's mother at the mall on Sunday when I was picking up a card for your father's birthday and she just looked so sad. I felt so sorry for her. She didn't see me, which right now is a good thing, because I'm at a loss for words of what to say, except the ones that I've already said, which is that I'm so, so sorry for everything. Trevor was her world, like you are my world. But one thing about life, as certain as death, is that it is never fair.

Most of all, Lissy, when you come home, which I know you will, I hope you can take a little time to read this. My biggest fear besides losing you is that you might find this letter boring. But I want you to know that I wrote it because I love you. Your father loves you too.

Lissy, I love you, please come home.

Mom.

Trio

Unsure what to do, and thankful to be out of the holding facility, she walked slowly, the expansive Texas sky a breath of fresh air before her. The day was thick and humid, the stickers from the brush alongside the desolate dirt road finding a home upon her dirty socks. But she was happy. There would be a hearing and she would have to appear in court to answer the charges against her, but the fact that she was a first time offender would give her the opportunity to 'work' the program.

Fumbling around for her wallet, she tried to remember where she had last put it. There had been money in her purse, she was sure of it, over a hundred dollars, but her search returned only a half-empty pack of chewing gum, a hair brush, and her dead phone, which was of no use to her. She was surprised that the phone was still there, and the case that it was in, which was an original Leon de Claire. She had heard stories that the wardens in the county jail couldn't be trusted and how they would steal your possessions, and now she was sure of it.

But then again, thieves aren't that smart, or choosy.

Dying for something to eat, even in the midst another cramp in her stomach, she ambled quietly in the sticky, Texas air in the direction of El Paso. A rattlesnake made its presence known from somewhere within the dry brush and the wind blew gently, thinning the air, as the reality set in that she couldn't even catch a bus.

She had lost more weight at the holding facility, she could feel it, and as she tugged upon the baggy shorts to keep them from slipping down her rear, her blouse slipped a little further down her shoulders. Although it was hot, it was a bright, new, clear day in July, that should have been full of promise, but the thought of her junior year starting soon was something that she didn't want to deal with.

It was strange how everything had changed in the course of a couple of months, and how far she had slipped after being crowned class valedictorian. She hadn't planned her decline, it had just happened. Silent and lithe, like the approach of a leopard. She couldn't go home, she was too ashamed to face her parents, and although she missed her friends, she couldn't hang out with them because she couldn't call them. As another spasm rippled through her stomach, she vomited. If they kept up, she would have to seek medical advice.

Blind to anything but the open sky, she chose to ignore the symptoms, walking aimlessly. As she contemplated a course of action, the sun beat down on her. Burned, and without any sunscreen upon her, she stuck a thumb in the air. As a trickling of cars whizzed past without an offer, the diarrhea began, leaking miserably into her undergarments. Within minutes, it had soaked through her pretty flowered shorts, so she removed her panty and tossed it into the brush. Ignoring her exit and the sign to El Paso, she threw up the contents of her stomach again, as the cars continued to whizz by.

The sun was making her sick, she just knew it! She wouldn't be this sick if it wasn't for the sun. A little sleep and she'd be ready to face the world again, or at the very least Steven and her mother.

Thumb to the air, she continued walking, as the sun beat down mercilessly upon her. The next vehicle on the road rolled to a halt instead of streaking past her. She'd go anywhere right now, with the exception of El Paso. She just wasn't up to facing her parents yet, and she needed a fix.

As the window of the Lexus rolled slowly downward, a girl with tousled, honey hair greeted her with a smile. About 18, she flaunted a stunning, crimson ring that sparkled brighter than her smile. In the rear seat sat her two male companions.

"Let's roll," she said to Lissy, patting the seat beside her. "The boys in the back gave me the affirmative, so this seat has your name on it."

Tired of her aimless walking, Lissy climbed in beside the driver.

"The name's Scarlett," the girl said. "Like in O'Hara."

As Scarlett flashed the ring, the light splashed off her finger.

"Scar for short," the girl said. "I know, it's crazy, don't ask. I hope you're headed to South Padre, because that's where we're going."

"I'm headed up that way," Lissy said. "I'm headed anywhere but El Paso."

She stared at the large rock, trying to estimate its size and value.

"Well then, climb in," Scarlett offered, smiling back at her men. "It's summer, so get ready to roll, because we're headed there on vacation. It's a non-stop party, South Padre," she said, as Lissy kept her eyes on the stone. "It's where everyone's headed."

"That's a ten hour drive and halfway across Texas," Lissy answered.

No sooner did she protest, that the boys in the back roared in laughter.

"My parents will kill me." Lissy said.

They were, they were going to be double super duper furious.

She couldn't just head up there, party or no party; she had business to attend to, like charging her phone and scoring some meth. Or anything- whatever would get her wasted.

But a party on the island? She could meet some new friends.

Indecisive, she stared at the ring again. Scarlett was right, it *was* summer, and time was a wastin'. Her indecision caused another round of laughter.

"So- what's your decision then?" Scar said as the boys laughed.

Amid the laughter, she heard an echo from the leather.

"It'll be a blast and you know it," one of the boys said.

"You'll finally have something to write about in English class this September."

She glanced at the teen who had spoken; his athletic physique and sandy hair reminding her of Trevor. Although she didn't want to, she had to get past always seeing him wherever she went, as it just wasn't good for her.

Ignoring the handsome boy, she spoke to Scarlett.

"I'd like to, but how long are we staying?" Lissy asked.

Scarlett's disheveled waves of honey-baked hair caught the wind, as Lissy busied herself staring at the conspicuous stone again.

"I can't be gone forever." Lissy said.

Gosh! That rock was the shiniest rock EVER! She wanted it!

She wanted to be gone, but she couldn't. And then, there was the 'little' problem with the kids. Although they looked like nice kids and everything, Lissy doubted that they shot up meth.

"If you call a couple of days forever, then just forget it," Scarlett said, peering into the mirror and parting her mane so that it curved seductively along her chin. "We just want to party. And besides, I have to be back at work on Friday. Come on, spoil sport. Don't leave me alone with these two illiterates."

Her conversation elicited another round of laughter, as the other boy spoke up from the rear of the Lexus.

"Just for the record, I'm Jake, and this is Dallas," he said. "Say hello to the pretty girl, Dallas."

"The name's Lissy," she answered. "Short for 'Elizabeth, but everyone calls me 'Lissy.'"

As Dallas stared, he wound a lock of shoulder-length, chestnut hair tightly around a finger.

"I'm from El Paso," Lissy said.

"We never would have guessed," Jake chortled as Dallas loosened up to join him. "You just said that, remember?"

"Oh, right," Lissy said. "I did."

She was beginning to feel a little better; making small talk with kids her own age was therapeutic for her. Relaxing for the first time since before her confinement in Alta, she made her decision. It was abrupt, to be sure, but those were the best. The smell emulating from the Lexus was one of Scar's perfume and leather as she voiced a dare.

"Let's do it," she said. "Sixty bucks says that it's going to take at least ten hours to get down there."

"Wrong," Scar sang, revving up the motor. "Sorry, lady. Eight hours or under; I made this trip last summer."

With the push of a jeweled foot to the pedal, she spun the vehicle back onto the near-empty highway, as Jake's husky voice broke the silence.

"We're from Albuquerque," he said, as Lissy breathed in the sweet scent of perfume and leather. "That's a ways past El Paso."

"El Paso High," she said. "Home of the one and only Steers. I'll be a junior when school starts back up in August."

"August 7th," Jake sighed, extending a hand to her. "I'll be a junior, too, and these two punks will be seniors."

Envious of his older friends, his strong hands raked through his mop of wheat-colored hair as Dallas stuck his tongue out at her.

"Lucky suckers," Jake said. "I'd give anything to be a junior this year."

"August 20th," Lissy offered. "I guess that gives me more time to party."

"That it does," Scarlett sang, tapping a polished finger to the window in nervous chorus. "Say, you wouldn't happen to have a cigarette, would you? I'm dying for one, dude."

"Same here," Lissy said as the boys smiled. "I haven't had a smoke in days and I've got the jitters like you wouldn't believe. I almost forgot what it's like to inhale!"

Her comment eliciting round of laughter elicited as Scar veered the Lexus off the next off-ramp of the highway.

What she wouldn't do for a cigarette. Or some meth. It had been days, and she was craving it something bad.

Lissy stared out the window as the Lexus rolled across the desolate desert, picturing Trevor again.

You've got to stop this. It's not good for you at all. Besides, your new friends are going to think that you're pretty weird.

Pulling the car off the road at a lone pump masquerading as a station, Scar positioned the Lexus alongside a rusted propane tank, turning off the motor.

"Marlboro menthol-milds?" she sang, although it was more of a statement than a question. "I'll be back in a second."

Emerging from the antiquated road stop seconds later, she tossed Lissy the telltale carton.

"It's your lucky day," she chortled in a stiletto voice as Lissy opened the pack of smokes with her fingernails. "They had your menthol, darling. Now, that makes four of us hooked on these coffin nails."

95

Chuckling, Lissy lit up and inhaled the sweet smoke deep down into her lungs as Scar, sandaled foot to the floorboard, accelerated the Lexus back up onto the highway. The nicotine was making her feel like herself again, and the boys in the back had fallen asleep, leaving only Scar to converse with.

"I thought those two jokers wanted a smoke," Lissy said.

So strange that they both had passed out.

Scar winked at Lissy, looking at her arms.

"Since you asked, the boys prefer meth," Scar said. "Although I'll take my cocaine in any form. Will a few hits of blow have you feeling better, Lissy?"

Her secret out in the open, Lissy took another long drag of the cigarette. Her addiction had obviously become apparent, which wasn't good. She had been wrong about the kids, though, and the fact that 'c' was in the picture lifted her spirits.

"Your tracks," Scar whispered, placing a finger gently upon a bruised vein in Lissy's arm. "I'm not a mind reader, although I have been accused of it."

Embarrassed, Lissy tried to ignore her.

"I have them too, Lissy. See?" Scar said. "Our unfortunate, visible 'friends.'"

Pulling up the sleeves of her sweater, Scar held out her arms.

"All the good veins are taken," she laughed softly, pulling the sweater back down to conceal the track marks. "So now I go with the toes. And I bet that you do, too. You know, Lissy, what really gets me down is that I have to wear sleeves all summer, no matter how hot it is. What about you, Lissy? What bothers you? Anything?"

"Definitely sleeves in the summer," Lissy said, opening up again. "But it doesn't keep me from getting high, Scarlett."

"I know," Scarlett answered softly, as the rear seat squeaked. "I think that's another reason that the boys and I picked you up, because you're an addict. What gives?"

"You couldn't tell that," Lissy said.

How dare she accuse her! Of all the nerve!

The commotion had awakened Jake, who had made it his job to listen.

"No worries," he said, reaching across the seat to tug playfully at Lissy's silky hair. "Dallas had you pegged for a tweaker, and Scarlett for a junkie, but I was right, because I guessed meth. The purer, the better, I would guess. Right, Lissy? Now, hand that carton of smokes back here!"

With another playful tug at her hair, he grabbed the carton from her hands.

"Hey! Give me a pack!" Lissy said.

"Not a chance," Jake answered. "Not unless you fess up that you're just as messed up as we are."

"I confess, I confess," she said. Now, hand me a pack!"

Now, it was Dallas who jumped up, a cigarette between his lips, in search of a lighter.

"Does anyone have a light?" Dallas asked. "I'm speaking to you, people. So get on it."

Playful, like his 'twin,' he smiled bashfully as she lit the cigarette for him, and then offered her a piece of candy.

"I'm glad I'm here with you goof-off's," Lissy said, sucking on the candy. "I mean it. I haven't laughed this much in awhile."

"We have something even better than laughs," Jake said. "It'll keep us happy until we get to the island, and that little something is right here in my pocket, baby. It's a 'shroom,' he said, growing quiet as he pulled the mushroom from his pocket. "Here, try this."

He tossed Lissy the mushroom, as she caught it, chewing it thoughtfully. She had never had a 'shroom' before, which bothered her, but just a little bit.

"One's my limit," Lissy said. "I like my hallucinations mild."

As she swallowed the foul- tasting mushroom, Jake popped one into his mouth, and then tossed Lissy another.

"Down the hatch," he said as she swallowed it.

"Your turn, Dallas, my man," Jake laughed, throwing one to Dallas.

With a single gulp, Dallas followed suit, and Jake sunk sleepily into the leather.

"This boy from Albuquerque is tired, so wake me when we get there, Scar."

Paying Jake no attention, Lissy laughed as Scar peeled out around another corner, dust flying behind them. With Jake out like a light, Lissy tried to talk to Dallas, but she was too late, for he was sleeping.

"Men," Scar chuckled, pressing the pedal to the floorboard. "What would we do without them?"

"Rule the world," Lissy whispered, the mushrooms taking over. "We would rule the world, Scar."

Like the boys, she, too, was slipping into a world that was better. A moment ago her mouth had had that 'tinny' feel and her panties were wet with diarrhea, but after the 'shroom,' she was flying where no one could get to her. Her dope sickness had been replaced by the seductive scent of citrus and leather, intermingled with strands of translucent pearls which hung before her. Reaching out for one of them, she groped blindly at the leather.

"Silly pearl," she said, as it floated past her.

Straining to catch one of them, she leaned over. Bleary- eyed and without success, she reached again, coming up empty handed, as the elusive treasures floated away from her.

"I can't catch the pearls, Scar," she said.

Her eyelids were heavy, and she was tired.

"Will you catch one for me? Because I can't find them."

The gems shimmered elusively above her- shimmering, bright, rainbow jewels, and she adored them.

"Just one, Scar," she said. "If you catch just one pearl for me, I won't ask you another thing."

"Somehow I doubt that," Scar said, her laughter wind chimes in the Texas air as Lissy flailed her arms wildly in her search for treasure.

"Anyway," said Scar, "I'm driving, so you'll have to keep on trying."

"Scar, it's raining pearls of brilliant colors," Lissy whispered, slipping down a little further into her seat. "Aren't they beautiful, Scarlett?"

As Lissy relaxed, her head began nodding. When she looked up again, Scar and the boys were talking, and her brilliant treasures were gone.

"Ouch," Lissy said, feeling her head. "Your 'shrooms almost did me in, Jake. Talk about a headache!"

She didn't need more problems. And her stomach was lurching again.

"Scar, pull over," Lissy said. "I think I'm going to be sick."

As Scarlett whipped the Lexus off the highway, Lissy moaned and clutched her stomach.

"Jake," said Lissy, "you made me eat that second mushroom, so you can clean up the vomit."

"Not in this lifetime," Jake answered, lighting up a cigarette as Scarlett veered the Lexus off into a patch of scrub brush. "I mean, you know I love you and everything, but when it comes to vomit, I'm afraid that's where I have to pass."

Ignoring him, Lissy stumbled from the vehicle and threw up in the weeds.

"Ugh," said Dallas, watching. Mortified at the sight of it all, he had turned a lighter shade of pale.

"I can see why you have a weight problem, Lissy," he said.

"I don't," she said defiantly. Yet it was an insult that she had heard many times before.

"I actually want to lose a few pounds, Dallas."

How long had it been since she had shot up some meth? Two days? 24 hours? No matter, because her dope sickness was becoming worse, and she would have to see a doctor.

"How long until we get there?" She asked Scarlett.

It was agony to have to climb back in the Lexus, but she did it.

"Dude, you've got it bad," Scar said. "I'm really sorry. A couple of hours. Can you make it, honey?"

More than just a little bit queasy, Lissy rested against the headrest. "Then step on it, driver. I can sleep when I get there."

The sun's position in the sky signaled that they'd been on the highway for hours.

"Say, what time is it?" she asked to no one in particular.

It had to be around 5, give or take an hour.

"Time to solve all of our problems," Jake laughed. "It's three o'clock, Lissy."

"This has been the longest day," she said. "I wish I felt better."

She did, there was no denying. She was quickly growing tired of feeling sick every day, and of being nauseous and sleeping through most of them.

"Want another 'shroom, Lissy?" said Dallas.

"Sure," Lissy answered. "Like in another lifetime, maybe. But I'll take an aspirin if you have it."

"Catch," Dallas offered, tossing her a tablet. "I come prepared."

She looked at the pill, which had landed on the floor. It was large and round, and didn't look like aspirin.

"That's not aspirin," she said. "I wasn't born yesterday, in case you didn't notice."

The three jokers were beginning to wear on her nerves, what little she had left.

"It's a Vicodin, Lissy," said Scarlett. Its 800 mg and you need to take it. Besides, it's just one tablet."

"So was the 'shroom,' Lissy answered. "And look where it got me."

Her skin was crawling and she felt lethargic. Not only that, but the dull pain in her left temple had migrated to the right, and her hair smelled like vomit.

"If you didn't take the 'shroom, you'd be sicker, you can bet on that," said Jake. "Admit that we did you a favor."

"Whatever," Lissy said.

She was tired of arguing, and maybe the painkiller would really help her.

"Don't wake me up until we're there," she said to Scarlett. "Unless we shoot up, and that's an order."

"Will do," Scarlett answered, laughing as she tossed back her mane of disheveled curls. "Get some sleep, my friend. You'll need it for what's coming."

A frown on her otherwise smooth face, she grew silent.

As the sun sank low in the vast Texas sky, Lissy stared out the window, trying to take her mind off her problems.

What was her mother doing this sultry, summer afternoon in the height of summer? She had to be frantically searching for her. She hated that she was worrying her parents needlessly.

As long as she wasn't calling the authorities to intervene. That would be a bad thing. And her father worried even more than her mother. She could see him now, pacing back and forth in the office, telling his secretary to cancel his afternoon patients. Between the two of them, their concern could tie up the phone lines from El Paso to Albuquerque. But it was her fault. She was certainly an official runaway. She'd call them. First thing in the morning.

Feeling the effects of the Vicodin, she slept like a newborn calf for several hours before waking to laughter.

She never knew that she was so incredibly funny! But evidently she was.

"Dude, I wish I could sleep like that!" said Dallas, waking up from his own nap. "What's your secret, Lissy?"

"I've been sick, remember?" she answered.

A cigarette was hanging from his bluish lips, and he looked wired.

"Dallas, pretty please pass me another one of those coffin nails?" Lissy asked. "From the pack that Jake stole from me, partner."

Groggy, but feeling slightly more human, Lissy sat up and looked behind her. Jake was awake, tuned in to his IPod;

and Dallas' lips just kept getting bluer. Lighting up the smoke, she let the nicotine sooth her fears.

"Look, how much further?" Lissy asked. "I really do hate to be the bearer of bad news, but this ride is getting a little ridiculous."

She looked around her, seeing nothing familiar. While she had been sleeping, the landscape had changed from one of grassland and cactus, to water.

"We're on the island," said Dallas. "And that great big body of water that you see out there is Laguna Madre."

"Ah," she said. "That explains it."

The water was a welcome change from the fierce heat of the desert, and didn't make her lungs burn. She had been here, but it had been a long time ago, when she was just a child.

"I know that, Dallas," she said. "I was here as a child."

"Get ready to rock and roll," Scarlett said. "It's time to party."

Scar drove the Lexus with a vengeance now, as if every second mattered, which maybe it did. Inhaling the nicotine deep down into her chest, Lissy leaned back across the seat and poked Jake in the stomach.

"Hey, meth boy," Lissy said. "Wake up! Let's get this party started!"

She liked Jake, he was funny. In some strange way, he reminded her of Trevor.

Remembering her soiled and ill-fitting attire, she choked on the cigarette.

"Whoa, look at what I'm wearing," Lissy said to Scarlett. "This is all I have, so dressing up is out of the question."

She had never looked more disgusting and dirty in her life. But then again, it wasn't every day that your best friend died right in front of you.

"This isn't some fancy dance party," said Scarlett. "So, relax, Lissy, because your clothes don't matter."

All smiles, Scarlett blew a kiss in her direction.

"You look fine, lady," said Scarlett. "So just enjoy it."

"Right," Lissy said. "I get it."

The narrow strip of land that they were driving on was becoming even smaller, a stretch of fancy hotels, white sand, and pavement surrounded by water, as the Lexus purred along as if it belonged there.

"Who are your friends?" asked Lissy. Do they live on the island?"

The long, narrow stretch of land was a curious place, and there was no one upon the pavement.

"It's a vacation rental," said Scarlett. "A group of kids from school rented a big house for the summer, and they're cool with us coming down here. You'll like them," she laughed, flinging back a strand of honey hair. "There'll be some underclassmen, but most of the kids are seniors."

"Any hot prospects?" Lissy asked. "I need a boyfriend."

What she needed wasn't a boyfriend, but a needle to her forearm, and a distraction from her illness.

"Please tell me that there will be at least a *few* hot dudes, Scar," Lissy said.

She had voiced her concern with a smile, but couldn't have been more serious.

"Well?" Scarlett asked, turning behind her. "What should we tell her? Will there be any 'hot prospects' for our new friend here?"

Before she could finish her sentence, the back seat came alive with laughter.

"You're looking at him," Jake said. "Signed, sealed, and delivered. Take me away on your spaceship, Captain Lissy!"

"Wow," Lissy said. "Thanks for the offer. I'll think about it."

She loved bad boys. And nice boys, too. She really did.

Leaning over the seat again, she slapped Jake's thigh playfully.

"Remind me again when we get there, would you?" Lissy said. "And I just might take you up on it."

With his halo of sandy hair and solid shoulders, he was reminding her more of Trevor by the minute. It was too bad that she was into meth, and not sex. The worst thing about meth, other than the withdrawals, was that it took away your sex drive once you were really into it. Which could be a good thing, as it kept her mind on the business at hand. But Jake, he was a looker, just like Trevor.

As she breathed in the invigorating aroma of salt and island water, she thought about how wonderful it would be to just have a little sex every now and then, just to get the blood pumping.

"I love the ocean," Lissy said to no one in particular. "I feel at home here."

She did, she wasn't lying. She had always loved the ocean, ever since she had been a young girl growing up in Austin. A big reason that she had balked at the move to El Paso. Corpus Christi would have been a better choice, as it was closer to the water.

How could an ocean girl be expected to acclimate to the desert? Why did her parents do that to her? What was wrong with them? She was a mermaid out of water. It was no wonder that she had taken up meth.

Whereas the narrow peninsula had been dotted with pretty little cookie-cutter houses, now they were becoming more distinctive and larger, as Scar left one street for another, and then another. The peninsula was now alive with vacationers, some with deep, dark tans, and others who were lazily working on them. Most of the women were wearing wide-brimmed hats and sunglasses, and the men the stereotypical flowered shirts and sandals. Lissy laughed heartily as the houses grew larger and the island smaller, the boys trading jokes for her affection. With a jerk of the wheel when the road was at its end, Scarlett veered the Lexus off the pavement. The home behind the white wood fence was tall, yellow, and stately, gaily painted to match the surrounding flowers and spirit of the island.

"Appearances can be deceiving," Scarlett interjected as Lissy stared at the monstrosity before her. "Outside might spell 'mom and pop,' but inside is one big party."

As Lissy climbed from the car and stretched her legs, she listened to the sounds emulating from behind the open door- an explosive blend of rock and roll intermingled with hearty laughter. Knocking lightly and without waiting for an answer, Scarlett entered as Lissy followed behind her. From the moment that she stepped over the threshold she was in another world, one of dancing and carefree abandon. Mesmerized by the scene before her, she clung to Scarlett's hand as the girl with the honey hair whirled her into the midst of it.

"Grab a beer," Scarlett demanded, swiveling to the rhythm and placing a plastic cup beneath a spigot to pour herself a tall one. "Is your fancy Salvator, or Sam Adams?"

As Scarlett swayed to the rhythm, beer in hand, her violet yes grew cloudy. "Dance, Lissy," she murmured, her hips feeling the rhythm. "It's summer."

"Summer," Lissy whispered, following Scarlett's lead and placing a cup beneath a spigot. "That it is."

As she surveyed the churning sea of teenagers, she searched in vain for Jake and Dallas. The home had three levels, and there were just too many people to try to find them.

"Say, Scar, what happened to our men?" Lissy asked her. Attempting to get her attention, she gyrated to the music until Scarlett turned to listen.

"They're big boys, Lissy, they can take care of themselves," Scarlett answered, as Lissy took another sip and glanced around her. "Big boys that love a good party."

Every available nook and cranny of the spacious home was teeming with dancing, perspiring people, the walls vibrating in motion. Feeling the beat, Lissy danced through the crowd, beer held high above her. She was glad she had come here. And she was feeling better. Draining the last drop of liquid from the cup, she poured another.

Scar couldn't have been more correct that they were going to get high here!

Sailing lithely through the sea of faces, she searched for Scar, who had also disappeared.

"Follow me," Scarlett sang, appearing out of nowhere and taking hold of her wrists to lead her toward the basement. "I promised you some good action, and it's time to make good on the promise."

"Sounds like a plan," Lissy said, letting Scarlett drag her along. "I want you to introduce me to your friends, the ones that you keep raving about."

"Which is why we're on our way down to the basement," Scar said, keeping a firm hold on Lissy's wrists until they had reached the bottom of the stairs. "Beer's alright, Lissy, but its 'c' we're after."

The lower level of the home dark, Lissy struggled to see. As Scarlett gyrated over into a corner of the dimly-lit room, she followed suit, sliding beside her upon the sofa.

"I told you we'd make it!" Scarlett said to the group upon the sofa as Lissy's eyes widened. "James, Brent, Alexis, Sandra, everyone- this is Lissy. She's from El Paso."

As Lissy watched the cocaine being melted down around her, Scarlett smiled broadly. Wasting no time, she pulled a shoelace from her pocket.

"Catch," Scarlett sang, tossing Lissy a shoelace held together with a slipknot at the bottom. "Time is a wasting, girlfriend."

With a smile as soft as the candles around her, Scarlett winked at Lissy, then injected.

"Your turn," she slurred slowly. "This stuff is pure Heaven."

Thrilled that the party involved meth, Lissy slipped the shoelace around her arm, and reached for the needle. It was all exactly like Scarlett had promised. The island, the house, the mood, the music, the people... Only the liquid gold before her could perfect the otherwise perfect scenario. Her vision hazy, she slipped in the needle. Within seconds, her muscles had relaxed and euphoria had set in, as she breathed in the sweet scent of weed all around her.

Ah, Mary Jane and meth. A party to remember. One that would heal what was ailing her and make her feel good.

"Sisters?" she mumbled dumbly to Scarlett. "I can't thank you enough for inviting me here, I feel like I've known you forever."

In her euphoric heaven, she leaned back and looked around her. Save for the light of the candles, everyone's face was near indistinguishable in the darkness, as she smiled numbly at a copper-haired boy beside her. His lips were moving, and he appeared to be talking to her, yet she couldn't hear a word he said. In a gesture of goodwill and friendship, she laid a hand upon his.

"Sisters," Scarlett seconded, her voice a whisper. "For ever and ever."

Like the boy with the copper hair, Scarlett was speaking, but Lissy couldn't hear, her mind drifting in the smoky air. Grinning dumbly in his direction, Lissy smiled broadly for his benefit. His face was animated, and his lips fluttered wildly, yet no sound emerged, at least not one that she could decipher. Giving up on what might have been an awesome conversation, she laid down, head in the boy's lap, at one with the world around her.

There was plenty of time to get to know Scarlett's friends, she had an entire summer ahead of her, and now she had an excuse to hit the road to New Mexico next summer. As the sea of faces above her grew cloudy and the boy with the copper hair lit a cigarette, she yawned, and then took it away from him to place it between her lips.

So good. So good. So damn good. Ah, summertime. Summertime and meth. She never wanted the feeling to end.

It was a perfect world, this land of perfume, meth, candles, and leather, and she was glad to be a part of it. Ah, and the boys! They were the best part yet!

As the music grew louder and the smoke from the marijuana swirled around her, she passed out in the lap of the boy with the copper hair.

Bourbon and Toulouse

The next day started out like the evening prior, as she got to know the boy with the copper hair a little better. Seventeen and a junior in September, he attended Albuquerque High with Scarlett and the others. A member of the wrestling team since his freshman year, he sported a muscular physique and 'six pack' that Trevor would have died for. Between melting down meth and shooting it up, she lit cigarettes in the basement, engrossed in conversation with the bulky wrestler.

Since her arrival on the island, the meth had flowed freely, and according to Zack, her new-found friend, was strong on continuation. Whereas she would be leaving in the morning with Scarlett; Zack, along with Scarlett's two cohorts and most of the others, was staying on.

"Just stay another week," Zack said, as they injected. "I really want you to stay so that we can continue the fun."

His taffy-green eyes begged her to reconsider, as she laughed off his request and thought about her current situation.

"I can't," she answered, as his eyes grew smaller. "As much as I'd like to, Zack, I can't, because of practice. Cheer, that is. It starts up again at the end of August and I need to start practicing for it."

She would have given anything to stay and party at the leased residence which she had christened the "Meth House," but by now Steven and her mother must be worried sick about her. And she still hadn't called them. Wondering why she was becoming such a thoughtless daughter, she lit up another cigarette, blowing the smoke in Zack's direction.

"Say, can I use your phone?" she asked. "My mom and dad have probably already put out an all-points bulletin on me because I haven't called them."

As the answering machine kicked in, she left a long-winded message about how she had gone to visit some old friends the next town over after being released from Alta, and would be home shortly.

"That should satisfy them," she said, as the taffy-colored eyes softened. "Although I want to, I just don't feel like going home yet."

"Then don't," Zack answered, looking longingly at her. "It happens to the best of us. My folks have no idea that I'm hanging down here. If they did, they'd ground me for the rest of the summer for sure. After they killed me. No, seriously, Lissy, I gave them what they wanted to hear, and told them that I'm staying with friends."

"Of course," she breathed slowly, her head spinning as she injected the meth. "It happens."

As she leaned back against his shoulder, the coughing began.

"Hey," Zack said as he stroked her hair. "You should really check that out. It sounds bad."

"There's always a buzz kill somewhere," she answered. "Look. It's nothing. But I appreciate your concern. I've been coughing forever."

"Well, forever is a long time," Zack said, not willing to let it lie. "So how long have you really been shooting meth? Your secret's safe with me, Lissy. I have my own demons. It's not something I'm proud of, or that I routinely tell everyone, but I've been shooting up cocaine in since I was 12, which is almost 5 years. Let me give you a little bit of advice, because it makes a difference. Confine your usage to weekends, and maybe your cough will settle down a little bit."

Zack's expression was one of worry, and Lissy could tell that he really seemed to care, but she wasn't ready to fess up to anything yet. When she wanted to stop, she would. And that was that. Giving Zack the finger, she lit another cigarette.

"Helps with the coughing," she said.

It wasn't anyone's business how long she'd been using. Not her parents, not her friends. No matter who they were, or how much they seemed to care.

Annoyed, she took another long drag before blowing smoke rings into the air.

"Okay," Zack said. "Have it your way, Lissy. I said my peace. But that doesn't mean that I'll stop worrying about you, even after you leave here. I had a friend who died after coming down with pneumonia from a dirty needle last year. It still hurts."

"My best friend died this summer," she said. "Right there in front of my eyes, and there was nothing I could do about it. He shot up bad meth, Zack. It was horrific, you have no idea. It happened while we were in Juarez together. I put a rose on his casket at his funeral."

Talking about Trevor again was making her incredibly sad, and she couldn't deal with it.

"The grass hasn't even grown on his grave yet," she said, wiping away the tears. "Let up, Zack, you aren't the only one with problems."

As she drifted, her mind wandered. She really wanted to stay, but she couldn't. This boy was nice, different from the rest. She was enjoying their conversation, something that hadn't happened since she and Trevor had been together. Although she just wanted to be friends, she wanted him to know that she cared.

With a whistle, Scarlett entered the basement.

"Hey, lady," said, slurring her words and losing her balance as she clung to the railing. "I hate to be the one to crash the party, but we're leaving first thing in the morning. You know, that thing called 'work?'"

"Sure," Lissy said, as Scarlett lost her footing and fell down the stairs. "I'll be up before you even go to bed. Say, are you alright, Scar?"

"Never felt better," Scarlett slurred, picking herself up. Just keeping the party rocking. Goodnight, Lissy."

"Goodnight," Lissy said, glancing at Zack again.

He was snoring, deep in dreamland, copper hair upon her lap. She stroked his hair, thinking about how much she was enjoying this. But for everything that was right about Zack, one thing was wrong. She wasn't hooked on meth; her usage was just a weekend thing. And her cough wasn't bad. He was just envious, and couldn't handle the high yet. She continued fondling the copper hair as Scarlett left the basement.

"Sleep while you can," she murmured to him. "It will build up your resistance, my dear."

She lay there, just enjoying the silence and stroking his hair, inhaling the sweet, pungent air of the basement. It was a mixture of perfume and marijuana, which Jake and Dallas were smoking on the floor above her. She closed her eyes, rubbing Jake's neck, listening to the muffled laughter coming from the far end of the basement, and to the familiar popping sound of cocaine being melted down into meth. She wanted to stay forever, with the boy with the copper halo of hair.

Ah, the Meth House. She would most certainly be coming back. Back to the house. Back to Zack.

Fading in and out of sleep, stroking Zack's hair, she started worrying again. Her father, always one to be on top of things, would be cutting his days short at the office, reducing his patient load, to get to the bottom of her disappearance. No doubt he had been on his way to pick her up at the gate when she was released from Alta, and she hadn't been there. And for how her mother was handling it, well, just thinking about what she must be going through made Lissy cringe.

Why did parents always have to spoil all the fun? Why couldn't they just let kids be kids? Certainly, after they listened to her phone call, they would call off the search, and let her make her own decisions.

She was going to be eighteen in a year! So what was all the fuss about anyway? What difference did a year make? All that she was doing was making friends. And she just wasn't ready to go back.

The more that Lissy thought about it, she was embarrassed. Embarrassed about her stint in Alta, and not ready to talk about it yet. When she was ready to open up, to go home, well, she would go, and that was that. Because, the moment that she was back, not only would her parents force the issue of her disappearance, but all of the pain and hurt over Trevor's death would return, exposing wounds which were still too fresh.

The worry getting to her, she drifted over to the other end of the basement and worked her way into the huddled group of kids. It was way too early to shoot up again, but she didn't care. She yearned to end the pain which had overtaken her since that night at the bridge, and since Trevor's death.

They were supposed to live forever, she and Trev! They were kids! Kids don't die young! And especially not from poisoned meth.

As she guided the needle into her skin, the creamy liquid coursing through her again, her fears slowly dissipated, and the noise lessened in her head.

"I'm not ready to head back," she whispered to no one in particular. "Not yet."

She padded softly back to her spot on the sofa, and to Zack, who was still sleeping. When the nightmares came again, Trevor ablaze in the field, she kissed his check and went upstairs.

Unable to sleep, Lissy left. The house was dark and quiet, and even the gulls weren't awake yet. Leaving a note for Scarlett beside her bed, she thanked her for her friendship, promising to return. The stomach pains and nausea was coming back, and she was sick, and scared. With a last glance at the big old house, she headed up the road again.

She'd miss Zack the most, for his funny laugh and copper hair. And because it felt so right when he laid his head upon her lap. Thoughts upon Zack, she walked calmly up the street without a destination in mind, breathing in the salty island air.

South Padre was another world, a little strip of land separated from everyone and everywhere, a world which took her back to a happier place and time, and she had enjoyed it. She would come back to party here next year, and would stay longer. She walked until she came to a train station; the sun beating down upon her shoulders, then boarded the next train to head in the opposite direction from Texas. She didn't know where she was heading, and she didn't care. Anywhere that would place some distance between herself and the stately ranch house with the For Sale sign in front of it would work.

Seven hours and nine towns later, she debarked in Galveston to stroll alongside the ocean again, the gulls squawking their annoyance.

So close to home, but yet so far. And headed in the opposite direction.

Although it was afternoon, it was still a perfect July day and the weather was growing warmer, high time to leave the vast state of Texas for anywhere. Spying a bus bound for the busy city of New Orleans, and just because she hadn't been there before, she pulled out some of the cash that Scarlett had loaned her, and boarded.

Her fare would take her past Galveston and the gulf of Texas into the heart of Mardi Gras, and the city that never slept. She had emptied her wallet for it, and if she wanted to keep on going after she got there, she would have to access a money tree, which was out of the question, or hitch. The compartment smelled stale, like old sweat, and the passengers ignored her, intent upon their business of staring off into the air. She took a seat beside a window, and did the same. As far as she was concerned, she had nothing but time-a lifetime to devote to everyone and everything, and considering what she had been through, she deserved the trip.

On the 275 mile trip, she watched the desert and the ocean roll by as she faded in and out of sleep, trying to forget. She wasn't worried about traveling alone, as the bus was pretty packed, but about trying to find her next fix.

Was she really hooked? Had Zack been correct? Was it impossible for her to say 'no' to meth? Was she sick?

As the old bus rolled through cities which smelled of scrub brush and forgotten air, she slept. She needed a fix, and she needed it bad. Eight hours and six buses later when the bell finally rang to announce the city's presence, she set foot in a land of stagnant water and stale air, efforts to recover from the hurricane which had taken her under without success. Abandoned houses littered the landscape, and steamboats cruised slowly upon the muddy Mississippi, as she headed aimlessly there.

Walking along a near-deserted street, she put her thumb up in the air to hitch a ride over the bridge to the district of the infamous French Quarter. Although the city had been hit hard by the hurricane, some of the businesses were still there, and as several cars rolled by without taking her up on her offer, suddenly, and just about when she was ready to give up, an ancient, badly-dented pickup skidded to a stop beside her. As it screeched to a halt, she couldn't help but notice the rust that had collected on the rims.

"Hop in," a boy said, amidst laughter. "That is, if you're traveling in this direction."

Peering into the truck, Lissy looked at the kids. Unlike Scarlett and her backseat drivers, the two teenagers in the old truck were unkempt and poorly dressed. Motioning for her to get in, the boy who had spoken to her ran dirty fingers through a mop of unruly, greasy brown hair. He reminded Lissy of a lizard, and reeked of marijuana.

Beggars couldn't be choosy about who they rode with, and she was out of money. Either she got in the truck, or walked herself nowhere.

"If you're headed over the bridge to New Orleans, then I'm there," Lissy said, studying the filthy vehicle and it's just as filthy occupants.

The floorboards were littered with empty beer cans, and she didn't feel like going to jail again.

"Hi, I'm Lissy," she said to the boy who had spoken to her. "It's short for 'Elizabeth.'"

Feigning a smile, she squeezed in beside the lizard boy.

"That's Kit," said the girl who was driving. "But everyone calls him 'Kitchen' because he eats everything put in front of him. He's a real blast," she said, knocking a hand playfully against his head. "And I'm Peyton."

While Peyton was talking, Lissy couldn't help thinking that she should have kept on walking. The city wasn't that far off in the distance.

"That's one dirty river," Peyton murmured, staring at Lissy while twirling a lock of raven hair. "Smelly, too, just like Kitchen. When he burps, you should get a whiff of the air in here! I have to get out the aerosol and spray it!"

Evidently Peyton considered herself to be funny, because she broke out into a fit of laughter, followed by a round of belching from Kitchen. They were both so disgusting that Lissy was ashamed of herself for ever taking them up on their offer.

"This is an afternoon just made for cruising," said Peyton, with another toss of hair. "So we're cruising for a bruising in Kitchen's clunker. Get it, Lissy? Or should I spell it out for ya?"

As Peyton broke out into another bout of laughter, Lissy felt sick to her stomach again.

What was she doing here? Zack was right, she had issues that she had to deal with.

"A little burp will do ya," Kitchen slurred, smiling at Lissy with a toothless grin. "Welcome to the den."

Was she imagining it, or were all of his teeth missing? This was one messed-up kid.

"Love me or leave me, baby," Kitchen said to Peyton. "It'll be a long time coming before I let you touch my marijuana again."

"Promises, promises, all made to be broken," Peyton said, flicking a hand to his head again. "Lissy, where are you headed to in this shithole of a city? Ever since the hurricane, we don't get many visitors up here. You've probably noticed that most of the houses are boarded up and abandoned. Not only that, but the whole place smells like shit. Just like Kitchen," she said with another slap to the boy's head. "Maybe one day, he'll take a shower. Right, Kitchen?"

"I'm headed as far as the bridge," Lissy said, ignoring Peyton's malicious comment. "I'm visiting an aunt who I haven't seen since I was a kid, and then I'm heading back home to El Paso. That's about it."

That was all they needed to know about her. The teens weren't funny, and were getting on her nerves. With kids like that, it was no wonder that New Orleans had been blasted by the likes of Katrina. It was a mean thing to think, and not at all like her, but she just couldn't help it. Trying to keep the peace, Lissy smiled thinly at Kitchen.

"Leave her alone, Peyton," Kitchen said, spitting on the floorboard. "Can't you see that she wants to keep her business private?"

In some strange way, maybe the two teens were just trying to be friendly, but she just wasn't into it. Riding in the front seat of the old truck beside them was making her feel like them- stupid, and dirty. And unlike Scarlett and the boys, these kids would never wind up being her friends. Plus, she was dope sick again, and needed to score some meth. Bad. And all these two jokers had on them was marijuana. Nope, this just wasn't going to work. It had been good for a mile or two, and a couple of bad laughs.

"My stomach is hurting again," she said, pretending to be sick. "It's cramping up on me, which means I need to take my insulin. Drop me off here, I'm out of it, so I'm going to have to call for an ambulance. I really appreciate the ride," she said as the truck spun to a stop at the outskirts of New Orleans. "Maybe we can do it again."

At the time she had appreciated it, but now all she wanted was to get out of the truck and get out fast, and away from these two kids. Maybe it was because she was dope sick, but she just couldn't take their nonsense any longer. Jumping from the truck, she forced a finger deep down into her throat as far as it would go to bring up the vomit. Being dope sick did have its advantages, one of them being her ability to bring up the contents of her stomach upon command. Saying her goodbyes and avoiding the pair's curious stares, she stepped quickly out into the early dusk of the evening and started walking, the truck screeching off in a flurry of dust along the riverbed.

It was becoming routine, her illness. And the crazy thing about it was that she couldn't help it, and didn't seem to care. The stomach pain, the nausea, the diarrhea- it was third grade in Professor Thornton's class all over again, a ceiling of dripping, lumpy wads of spit. Thankful to be back out on her own, she watched the truck disappear in the thick, Louisiana air. With no direction and nothing on her mind but scoring some meth and quieting the voices in her head, she walked briskly toward the city along the river. With each day that passed, she missed Trevor like mad and her childhood haunts of San Antonio. Parents could be just so- bad.

Although dusk was upon her, she was within eyesight and walking distance of the French Quarter, which was good, as she sped up her pace along the riverbed. In the thick reeds along the river, a raccoon hovered in search of its evening meal, and bats fluttered lazily through the humid night air. She was a little uneasy about walking alone along the river at night, especially in a strange town that she hadn't been to before, but there wasn't much that she could do about it. Somewhere soon, when she got just a little bit closer to the city, she would come across someone who could help her. Trying to keep her mind off her next fix, she thought about the damage inflicted by the hurricane four years prior. She had read about the disaster in her history book, and now she had a firsthand chance to really see it.

Even with all of the attempts at renovation, the town would never be the same again, as most of the businesses had folded up and left. She walked briskly through the outskirts of the sorry city, past the rows of deteriorating, abandoned houses. Flooded up to their rooftops in muddy river water, they had been left to rot in the humid Louisiana air. Only recently had savvy investors been narrowing in, in search of another bargain.

But it was New Orleans, and here she was, smack in the midst of it, in the infamous French Quarter, just like she had read, and she couldn't be happier. If she ever got married, she would have something to tell her kids.

Applauding her ability to ditch the two shifty kids, she walked along determined to score some meth and just enjoy her time there. There was always tomorrow. Except for Trev. When a bat swooped low over her head, she cried out in surprise, trying to swat it.

As she turned off Toulouse Street and onto Bourbon, the city came alive, the sound of jazz drifting past her. Desperate to score and trying to keep her mind of her dope sickness, she searched for a place to go in. She was determined to enjoy her stay here, and couldn't think of a better city to enjoy a beer. Besides, she had been itching for the longest while to use the fake I.D. that she and Trevor had purchased prior to their trip to Juarez. It listed her age as 23, which she thought was a real kick.

When she saw a bright yellow flag waving jauntily from a corner, she headed toward the near-empty dive bar. She had wanted adventure, and this very well could be it, as the two kids with the arrogant attitudes surely hadn't done anything for her. The building was old and built of brick, wildflowers poking their desert heads out from between cracks in the cement. As she stepped over the threshold, the aroma of alcohol and stale cigar smoke welcomed her in. Sitting down upon a stool, she ordered a beer and looked around her.

Her stomach churned as she sipped the double ale, which didn't help it. Ignoring the danger signs and ordering another, she listened to the jazz band work its magic on the scattered audience. She surveyed the scene, the mom and pop types in their t-shirts and ruffled collars, the kids just barely over the legal age, the vagrants, and the occasional tourist. She could score here, she could smell it. She could spot a meth head just by the way that he or she glanced at her.

For a Friday night, the small bar had a sorry audience, with stools left unattended around the home town band. Whenever someone called out a tune, the bar would come alive with the sound of jazz again, as she raised her glass to the music and drank her beer. She drank eagerly, inhaling the magic of the city around her, and as the smoke filled her nostrils, she nodded off into her beer. Snapping herself out of it, she left the comfort of her perch, searching the sea of faces for someone who could help her.

Meth, cocaine, crack, even heroin. If it was available, she would take it. By the time that she had finished the beer, she was thirsty for another.

It's knowing how to tell a coke head from a cop, what to say, and when to say it. And using feminine wiles wisely to get it.

Swiveling her hips, she made her way through the thin crowd casting glances of impure intent, positioning herself seductively on a stool in the corner.

Sometimes, being an addict had its advantages. And the fact that she was female put her at the top of the list.

Toying with her hair, she surveyed the crowd again, sipping on the beer, ready to give it another go. She had selected two likely candidates, and it was time to walk past them with a gentle brush to the shoulder. As she was getting up to do so, a stool was pushed beside her, and she looked up to see a weathered man in dirty overalls and a t-shirt with silver hair and leather skin. He was smiling at her, and holding out a beer.

Strange, the old codger had appeared out of nowhere. She hadn't seen him on her trip around the bar, but then again, she could have missed him. He didn't look like a meth head, but then again, neither did she.

Motioning for him to sit down beside her, Lissy took the beer. The old coot had made her search easy, which called for a celebration. Maybe, just maybe, he knew how to get his wrinkled hands on some meth. Raising her glass to his, she feigned interest in him and drank the beer. Within minutes, she had him believing whatever she said, as she moved her stool a little closer, playing upon his thirst for feminine attention. High on confidence and her need for meth, she worked him with her feminine wiles and closed in, asking questions about where she could score some meth.

"I wish I was a little older," she whispered into his ear. "Because this girl from Texas really knows how to show her man a good time."

In this dive, she could ask for the state of Texas and get it. The state of Louisiana, too. And all she wanted was a little meth.

She drank the dark liquid down eagerly, squeezing his hand and feigning interest. The old man knew where she could score, which she wouldn't have guessed. She was pushing things a little, coming on to him, this gross old codger, but she was desperate, and he was willing to help her. Groggy from all of the alcohol she had ingested, she kissed his cheek, anxious to get on with the business at hand.

"Let's do this," she whispered huskily, her lips close to his. "Let's get out of here."

For a girl who had never even had sex, she could be pretty convincing, but then again, she was addicted. And one thing about meth heads was that they really knew how to work it, and she was no exception. She kissed his cheek again as they guzzled the beer, walking arm in arm out of the bar when they were finished.

"I'm game for a good time next time I come back here," she said, giving him another kiss. "And I'm always game for meth."

Squeezing his hand, she hugged him as they strolled lazily down Bourbon. Apparently the lonely geezer knew a dealer who hung out not too far from the bar.

She had done it, she had scored. And she was good. Darn good. It was surprising what her parents hadn't taught her.

Walking on air, her throat dry in anticipation, she continued kissing his cheek and feigning interest in him. No doubt, it had been a long while since he had had any feminine attention, even holding hands. As they walked, hand in hand, she couldn't help thinking how upset that Trevor would have been if he knew what she was doing to score some meth. But there were things that she had never told him, like how she had to do this every now and then. As far as she was concerned, a little attention of this sort couldn't hurt.

Anxious to get to where they were going, she followed him down one filthy street after another. Just when she was feeling like a common whore, she grew dizzy and her vision blurred. Unsteady on her feet, she clung to the man's arm and cried out for him to help her. Ignoring her plea, he moved erratically down the street and onto another, deaf to her plight as she struggled to keep up with him.

Unable to see in front of her, she fell to the cement. Her 'pimp' had disappeared around the corner, and was nowhere near. She lay and cried upon the cobblestones as the queasiness set in. It was another bout of nausea, only stronger. Desperate for a fix, she struggled to her feet, ignoring her inability to see and the sharp pain in her head as she walked blindly back to where she had been.

But where was she? The old man had taken her down so many streets that she had no idea where she was, or how to get back. Where was the old bastard? What made him leave her like that? What was even stranger was that he had left without the cash that she had offered him.

The pain in her head becoming too much to bear, she fell to the pavement again, holding her head, as the vomit started. Five minutes later she had vomited out all the beer that she had put in, including her breakfast. She lay there in her vomit upon the cold stones crying out for help, but no one was there, the dark street now completely deserted.

She hadn't even asked his name, which wasn't like her. What was wrong with her lately? She didn't like herself like that.

Too dizzy to stand, she lay upon the cobblestones in tears, the pain in her head becoming worse. The sound of jazz had left the air, and there were no streetlights to soothe her torture, only darkness. Her head throbbing, she vomited again, calling out for the man with the silver hair.

What on earth was wrong with her? An allergic reaction to something that she had had for breakfast? It made sense. These days, she believed almost anything. If she had only charged her phone, things would be different.

When she vomited blood instead of beer, she couldn't control herself any longer, as thoughts that she might have been poisoned ran through her head.

But why? She didn't have any money. And what little she did have was still on her.

She was obviously bleeding internally, and in need of immediate medical attention. Dizzy from the loss of fluids and blood, she lay upon the deserted street crying and begging for help in the cold night air.

"Help me," she murmured, head to the pavement. "Help."

As she lost consciousness, the stench of rotted eggs in the air, her stomach burst. Mouth agape and face smashed to the pavement, she let out an agonizing shriek which went unheard. Unbeknownst to her, her parents had filed a missing persons report two days prior.

Blinded

The nervous man with the wide-brimmed *sombrero* drove along restlessly, paying no attention to anything but the Mexican music blaring from the dashboard of the antiquated van with the Mexico license plate. Dirty, desperate hands beat in time to *mariachis*, the stub of a cigarette hanging from a mouth ravaged by toil and age. The cement turned to gravel, and a turn was made. Grinding out the butt on a window, he spit into the sun and rolled it down all the way. The music was getting him in the mood for what he had to do and there was no time to waste, and he drove along the narrow highway as fast as the old van could carry its cargo of grain towards the tiny town barely on the map of the United States. The air was hot, and would only be getting hotter during this delivery.

There was no air conditioner, only a jug of warming water, flies floating upside down upon the surface, legs waving, beside a rag to wipe his face. Digging it out, he cooled his face, sucking in the moisture. It was 92 degrees and climbing, which wasn't a good thing. The air in the cab was already stifling and hard to breathe, and it wouldn't be much longer before he would have to get off the road and seek shade.

And then what would he do? He had a delivery to make. He was Eduardo, the traficante king. No delivery, no pay.

Just for a second, as the Texas sun beat upon his face, he thought about the ones who didn't make it and the graves that he had had to dig, and about how and when he would die, for it was only a matter of time until he messed with the wrong *tipo*. Life wasn't easy for a *traficante,* although he hadn't expected it to be. He had been chosen for the dangerous position over many others, and he was grateful. For each day, for each delivery. Besides, if he had to dig a grave every now and then, what difference did it make? It was no big deal, just more money in his pocket for his family.

To keep his mind at ease, he thought about his wife and baby daughter back home in Juarez, in a plywood hovel that served as the family home in the most dangerous region of Mexico, a town that was becoming more dangerous by the day. Only a few hours' drive away, now, with the sun blaring down, it seemed like a lifetime away. His baby girl's name was *Sueso*, and she had thick, dark curls and plump, cherry cheeks, and with the exception of a day's visit last year when his Lydia had driven her to Texas, it had been almost three full years since he had seen her, fearful of what might lay in store for him if he broke the pledge that he had made upon his initiation into the trade. It was the old timers of who he was the most afraid, men who, in their leather skin, and under government wing, guarded the city's impoverished and drug-ravaged streets with AK47's and blades. Although hardened to the violence of the streets, they did not take kindly to how the lowly *traficante* made his living. He was a catfish on the bottom rung of the trade, but in the minds of the old timers, as despised as the common drug dealer and cartel kingpin.

Wiping the rag against his face again to calm his nerves, he pictured his Sueso, almost three, hand pressed into her mother's as she bounced in glee to the open market where, hands upon a mango, she would suck the flesh loose from the seed before helping her mother carrying home a sack of fruit to eat. The image of his precious baby girl and of his wife back home in Ciudad greatly calmed him and was a beautiful thing, as he thought about the money that he was on his way to make, money that he would add to the family savings to leave Ciudad Juarez.

The money was the part of the job that made it all okay, for he was on his way to buying his family a better life upon one of the small *ranchitos* that ran alongside the banks of the Rio in Jalisco. Every now and then, after he had added to the savings and if there was any money left, he would send a package down to Juarez- some cans of food from the market, a blanket, a fan to replace the one that had given out the summer before. Thus far, this had been a profitable summer, and all seven of the *jovencitas* that he had transported had made it from Logansport through the humidity and heat, and he was happy. The job that he was on his way to complete would not only guarantee the safe relocation of his family, but food for the table of the coming winter, and bottled milk for his precious Sueso. But today, just like every other day that he had journeyed, the desert sun was great, and the temperature was still rising, even late in the day. With any luck, upon his arrival in Logansport by nightfall, the temperature would have decreased to a level which would make the journey safe.

He consulted the van's thermometer, running the rag across the plastic face in an effort to see the mercury. 94 degrees. He'd have to make a stop at the bank of the *Terrebonne* to fill the jugs in the rear of the van with water so that his precious cargo would stand a chance in the heat. If the *jovencita* was to remain alive through the three hour journey, it was imperative that he had enough water to douse upon her face. He could stand the heat, but then again, his face wouldn't be covered in burlap and duct tape, items necessary to conceal and silence his human cargo from any travelers and from the *policia*.

With the exception of one unfortunate *jovencita* who had suffocated two summers ago in the heat, he had kept his part of the bargain and had delivered his cargo alive and breathing, and had done it well indeed. The young *jovencita*, at 13, had been almost too young for the trade anyway, and for the life of a *bebe frabricante*. Although he had been punished with a severe beating, he had not had any fingers cut off and had been allowed to live, on the condition that it would never, *ever* happen again. Ever since that day, every delivery that he had made had been a good one, impeded only by an extra stop or two to douse his human cargo with water. Life for his kind and for a *traficante* could be lucrative indeed, and on most days he was happy, thinking about his family.

There were a dozen sacks of wheat in the car, and the *jovencita* would make thirteen. He had been stopped only once in the 3 years that he had been in the industry, the fear that set in deep as the lone *policia* poked and prodded each and every sack of grain until, right before contact with his human cargo in burlap, he had put a bullet in his face. The blood that had spattered had taken too long to clean from the seats, time that had taken away from the journey in the Texas heat, and the *chica* had not made it. Thinking back on it now, putting the bullet into the *policia's* brain was why the *traficante de reys* behind the operation's curtain had let him live, even though a *jovencita* had died that day. He had proved that he would not be taken down easy, and ever since his victory over the *policia*, he had kept a statue of the Holy Virgin Mary upon the dashboard of the vehicle to guide his journey.

As he drove, he pushed the rag to his face, but the vision of the dead girl and the one mistake that he had made remained, mocking him and interrupting his journey. One dead *bebe fabricante* was one too many, and he was grateful that he had been allowed to live, he had been lucky. After the *policia* had left, he had torn open the sack and ripped off the duct tape that had been covering the airways of the *chica* who had been so young and sweet, but the face that had gazed back at him had been vacant and chalklike, even after he had doused her with water. Dragging the limp girl from the van, still wrapped tightly in burlap, he had bent over her upon the grass, in an effort to get her to breathe.

"*Respirar*," he had urged her, kissing the statue of the Holy Virgin Mary. "Breathe."

With an ear to her chest, he had listened, but heard nothing, so he had pushed his hands down dumbly between her breasts, in an attempt to rouse life into her face.

"*Respirar, estupido jovencita*, breathe."

In fear and desperation, he had taken a pocket knife and run the blade gently into a vein, just a little, to make her scream. But no sound had the *bebe fabricante* made, and he had hurriedly dug a grave in a pocket of barren soil before the *policia* came, the grave only two feet deep. He had rolled the dead girl into the shallow grave, the burlap still covering her face, packing dirt over the young body good and tight with his shovel. Then, like a thief, he had stolen away. The beating had come that evening, outside of the bar in which he had stopped for a drink. With two severely bruised eyes and three missing teeth, he had been one very, very lucky *traficante*. Ever since then, and since the placement of the Virgin Mary upon the dashboard, he said an extra prayer for his safety every day.

Rolling another cigarette, he tried to push away the image of the dead *jovencita* by thinking about happier things, like his family, and about the money that he would be assured for this next *recoleccion*- money that would finally be enough to move them out of the war zone that was Ciudad and onto a *ranchito* somewhere safe.

When he saw the cattails which were growing alongside the highway, he jerked the van off the road and down into the dirt, driving to where the reeds met the stream. Filling the jugs with water, he loaded them into the back of the Chevy alongside the sacks of grain, on his way once more to the fertile soil and parish of *Terrebonne*. Once he reached the sleepy town that lay on the border of Louisiana and Texas, it was on to Mississippi and the small airstrip that served as an airport to greet the waiting plane and the *traficante de rey*.

As he drove, he tried his best to think about happy things, like his *precioso* Sueso's birthday, and her chubby, angelic face, as he turned up the music and sang along to the *mariachis*. The music helped to drown out the great hum of the cicadas as they clung tightly to the branches of the great oak trees in pursuit of a suitable mate. Although he hated the noise that they made, he was tolerant of the pesky creatures, for they had their rightful place in life and in the scheme of things, just like his deliveries.

Ah, but for another successful and profitable recoleccion, heat or no heat. Ah, but for the money.

Singing to the music, he pictured his beautiful Sueso, and how, if she was riding along with him now, her pudgy fingers would bounce in tune to the beat. It had been a long time since he had seen his family, which made him very sad. Plagued by guilt, he drove blindly, thinking only of his baby, his wife, and the money.

Ah, the young jovencitas and the money they would make for the traficante de reys! If he was but to receive just a small portion of it, what glorious things he could buy for his baby girl and family!

It was the young girls that the *traficante de reys* targeted, as the males of the species couldn't make any babies. As the sun climbed higher in the Texas sky and the temperature in the van climbed to 95 degrees, he picked up the pace. The *jovencitas* that he delivered could live a far worse life than that of a *bebe fabricante* for the *sucios viejos ricos,* their sole responsibility in life to bear pretty little babies. He was proud of the young *chicas* that he delivered, and of the money that he was able to send home to his family.

This traficante, he had it made. Life was good. And soon he would be going home to his family.

Rubbing his face with the rag and singing in the heat, he watched the desert brush give way to a landscape of sycamores and shade.

Bound at the hands and feet, Lissy struggled to move as the duct tape cut into her feet. With both hands tied behind her, it was difficult to make any headway. She had no idea where she was, or whether it was day or night, or whether her kidnapper, whoever he was, was anywhere around. Not only were her feet bound at the ankles, but her face was wrapped in tape, making it difficult for her to breathe. If it wasn't for a small space near her nose, she would have suffocated already.

Maybe she was dead, and she didn't know it. Her memories were vague.

She had some recollection of being in the French Quarter and of drinking too much, and of trying to score, but none after she had fallen down in the street. Wondering where she was and why, and fighting to breathe, she tried to remain calm and figure out a way to escape.

She would die, like Trevor. Bad things had a way of coming in twos and threes. And she didn't want to die today.

Fighting against time and unable to move her legs, she remained quiet, her cheek pressed to the cement, listening for anything that might give her place of imprisonment away. The air was hot and stale and she was burning up, and every time that she tried to move, it hurt to breathe.

She was going to panic, and suffocate. Who had done this? And why? She didn't have any money. Certainly not enough for someone to take.

Obviously, whoever had taken the time to kidnap her and tie her up like this had to have some pretty twisted plans in store for her, no doubt having to do with holding her hostage while robbing her parents of their life savings, after which they would either let her go, which wasn't likely, shoot her, or just let her lay there to suffocate. She didn't deserve this, but then, neither did Trevor. The thought of the phone call that would be placed to her parents made her sick to her stomach. She let out a scream- loud and long, her parents' horrified faces floating above her in the darkness. But it was impossible to scream because of the tape.

Where was she? Why had someone left her here? When were they coming back?

Unanswered questions plagued her as she fought with the tape, screaming a voiceless scream to call attention to her plight. Her throat was dry, and she was thirsty. And her cell phone had been taken from her because she couldn't feel it. Rolling and kicking, impeded by the tape, she thought about Trevor again, and her mother and father, and about "Charlie" the pet rabbit that she had played with as a child growing up in Austin. He was nibbling on lettuce as she played with him in the grass in the backyard of her childhood home. He nuzzled her cheek and she giggled, petting his velvety face.

Charlie! Come back! Please, Charlie! Don't go away!

As the beloved pet hopped away, frightened by her laughter, she ran after it to catch it, but the tape cut her cheeks and she couldn't breathe so she rubbed her face on the cement and Charlie was hopping away so she kept rubbing just as hard as she could so that she could breathe. The more she rubbed, the harder the tape stuck, and she knew that she was going to suffocate.

Charlie! Charlie? Where are you? Please don't go away! Charlie?

But Charlie didn't come back, and in her anguish, Lissy fell asleep.

The *traficante* drove on as the heat gave way to the last shadows of day, past the Texas towns of Corpus Christi, Galveston and Port Arthur, as the sycamore trees with their graceful leaves turned to fields of green and deep forests of pine, to a shady place where the Sabine River met the shore of Logansport, Louisiana, and to his final stop to pick up his delivery. It was finally cooling off; the temperature in the van 90 degrees, which meant that he would stand a chance at delivering the young *jovencita* to the airport alive. If she was listless upon arrival, instead of water, he would douse her in whiskey, kept sealed away in a jar in the glove compartment for emergencies. And if she woke during their travels, he would play with her a bit, offering her some cola or a cigarette, because that would him happy. He took pride in his *bebe fabricantes*, just like he took pride in his money, and in his family.

It was the least that he could do for the ill-fated young women, and as he maneuvered the van along the bank of the darkening Sabine, his weathered face cracked into a smile. He liked to take good care of his *jovencitas*, to try to bring a glimpse of hope to their desperate faces, if even for a minute, before the coming perils of their journey. If he had been younger and unmarried, and before her delivery to the plane, he would most certainly force sex upon her, at least a couple of times, and probably a lot more if she was a pretty young thing, but he was a married man with a family, and thoughts of his Lydia and precious Sueso brought his mind back to less evil things. But even if he wasn't married, sex with one of the *bebe fabricantes* was out of the question anyway, because if a *jovencita* tested positive for child upon her arrival in Makita City, not only would he not receive his money, but his throat would be cut by the *traficante de reys.* It was all part of the deal that he had made.

His job was simple- to deliver the *chicas,* and when they were "safely" in the city in the hands of the men who ran the trade, his money would be wired into a bank account in Ciudad, all two thousand dollars of it, and he would be free to walk away and spend it as he pleased. A white *jovencita* under legal age commanded a much greater sum of money than an older *jovencita* of over the age of 18, and a *jovencita* of any other ethnicity. But whether the *chicas* were European, American, or another race, the money wasn't nearly enough for what it took to deliver them to the *traficante de reys*, but a good *traficante* didn't complain.

Ah, it was a joyous day!

A white *jovencita* would make many good and beautiful babies, *bambinos* that were sellable, and healthy, and was easily "inducted" into the illegal trade.

Rolling another cigarette and wiping the fly-ridden rag across his face, he peered out the window, anxious to arrive to where he had been told that this newest *jovencita* would be awaiting his arrival. The *traficante de reys* were savvy to the tricks of the *policia* and knew that the risk of being discovered was great, no matter what precautions they took, which was why that for every new delivery there was a new meeting place. Once he arrived at the place where the girl was hiding, his credentials would be verified, usually by a barrage of pictures and questions, after which he would be prompted for the password that had been assigned this delivery. Then, after all of the fussing, he would be on to the meet the plane, and the last leg of his journey.

"*No tengas miedo, chica,*" he breathed. "Don't be afraid." "*Hay destinos peores que ser un fabricante de bebe para el Filipino ricos sucia.*" "There are worse fates than being a baby maker for the filthy rich Filipino hombres."

At peace with his obligations, the *traficante* kept the old Chevy purring at a steady pace along the darkened Sabine.

"*No pasara mucho tiempo ahora, jovencita.*" "It will not be long now, young lady."

"*Papa va a venir.*" "Daddy's coming."

Recognizing the ancient iron bridge that ran across the Sabine from the picture sent him by the *traficante de rey*, he eased the van onto it, whistling softly. This newest *jovencita* would be waiting his arrival at the humble and pious town of Logansport, Louisiana, at the defunct construction site of the town's new library, behind the Veterans Memorial. He could smell the money; almost taste it; the scent of the *jovencita* in the bathroom stall of the abandoned library crying out his name.

His bebe fabricantes were wild horses to be tamed, their scent fresh as hay. Ah, but for the babies they would make!

It was the thrill that kept him going.

Lungsod ng Angeles

East of the South China Sea and several hundred miles north of Manila, with a population of well over 300,000 and an ethnicity that daunted even the most liberal Filipino, the unlikely 'Angel of the Philippines' and human trafficking hotspot of Angeles City glowed like a neon thumb above the horizon. A first-class, highly urbanized city with expansive high rise views and one too many sleazy yet exclusive restaurants and brothels, it was home to a thriving baby-making and sex trade industry, masquerading under such legal entities as massage parlors, medical clinics, homes for unwed mothers, and mail order brides for sale. Here, beneath the beckoning lights and entrances to the brothels, women who had been taken unwillingly from their homes were conditioned and implanted with human embryos, while others made a man's every desire and fantasy come true. It was a business of sex, and birthing babies for money. With an economy that had evolved from a defense-based industry into one of legal and illegal entertainment, the 'businesses' had *turistas* or 'tourists' a plenty, as men flocked by the thousands annually to the northern city not only to tour the defunct Clark Air Base, the largest United States military headquarters outside of the United States, but to participate in the illegal sex trade and in fathering babies for money. Many of the *turistas* were pre-selected 'gigolos,' men of American, Australian, and European descent who had been personally selected by the *traficante de reys* to father infants for money.

Although the air base was defunct, and had been since the eruption in 1991 of Mt. Pinatubo, the trades still flourished, evolving from forced labor operations into the sex and baby-making rings of today, where the market for a fresh, young *jovencita* of child-bearing age was alive and thriving. Underage *jovencitas* between the ages of 14-17 were the most desirable; with white females who had never born a child at the top of the pay scale. The women were selected not just for their genes and physical appearance alone, but for their addiction to drugs and alcohol, as the substance abuse made the *chicas* compliant and easy to manipulate as well. Addicted to alcohol and illegal drugs, the operations greeted them on a grand scale, pumping the youthful bodies full of powerful pharmaceuticals and legal drugs that would take the place of the heroin, meth, cocaine, alcohol, and whatever else they had ingested back home. It was a horrific business; one which wore the young women physically and mentally down through implantation, fertility treatments, and servicing, or a combination of all.

The drugs that the *chicas* were given during detox and throughout the duration of their pregnancies to enhance their experience and assure their compliancy were selected carefully like the *jovencitas* themselves; pharmaceuticals which wouldn't affect the health of the growing embryo and child. Hustled in by greed-driven *traficantes* who possessed phony work visas for the *jovencitas* employment in the field of 'tourism,' the young women were whisked into a life of child-bearing and toil upon the aircraft's touchdown at the international airport of Diosdado Macapagal. It wasn't just babies that the young *chicas* were forced to bear, but the responsibilities of sex and toil as well, in fields, factories, and laundries in and around the city. All of the young *bebe fabricantes*, throughout the duration of their pregnancies, in addition to birthing a baby annually, were expected to excel willingly in the positions assigned them. It was only during the last two weeks and the final stages of pregnancy that a *jovencita* was allowed time off from the fields to prepare her body for the birth to come. The last two weeks were not met with anticipation at all, for along with an increase in 'medications,' to 'ease' their labor, the girls were expected to service the *turistas* who frequented the brothels, as the possibilities of an early labor was upped. More often than not, a *jovencita* would find herself back at the 'clinic' that had implanted her, struggling with an early labor and tears to her birth canal. Forced to comply or face death to themselves and their families, the young women kept their mouths closed and worked the brothels in whatever way told.

Traficantes like Eduardo were paid their meager share of two thousand United States dollars in a lump sum upon the *jovencitas* arrival, after which the girls were whisked off into a waiting vehicle that masqueraded as one of the city's medics. From there, they would be given a comprehensive medical exam and pharmaceuticals to begin their detox at the *Banal na Sanggol Medikal Klinika, or* 'Holy Infant Medical Clinic,' and others like it, known not so much for its reduced-fee medical services that it provided to the city's impoverished, but for the trafficking of addicted, yet otherwise healthy young women capable of birthing an annual child. The operation was a highly demanding, four-part process, one of implantation, fertility treatments, servicing, and after a period of ten years, selling the *jovencitas* out to the highest bidder.

If a *jovencita* passed the initial medical exam, which consisted of a pregnancy test, blood work, and a humiliating physical, she would be placed into the vehicle once again for the day long journey into the hands of the 'home' or brothel, and the *traficante de rey* who would monitor her detox for implantation of the first embryo. After the three week detox and cleanse, the women were taken back to the clinic for implantation of the single embryo, after which they were carefully and continually monitored for pregnancy as they toiled in the laundries and fields. The fertility window was narrow, one of 9 to 12 days at most, by which it was known if the implantation to the uterine walls had been successful. After the pregnancy testing, the *jovencitas* who were not with child were forced into a mandatory 12 month 'conditioning' schedule- one of thrice-daily fertility treatments to ensure an embryo. It was the lucky *jovencita* who could stomach the fertility drugs, as a live birth was quicker to result. Many a *chica* got down on her knees and begged that the treatments would result in multiple embryos, for if both the implantation and the fertility treatments failed, the *jovencitas* were put on a 'training schedule' and 'serviced out' to the random *turistas* who frequented the brothels, a fate that caused some of the women to try to escape from the brothels, or kill themselves. A *jovencita* in this final stage of the operation was forced to service dozens of men every day for a year upon command and around the clock for the purpose of pregnancy, while still toiling in the fields. The women in this final stage suffered intolerably and almost without sleep, as only two hours was given for 'time off' in a 24 hour window. The *bambinos* birthed in this despicable and random, impure fashion were considered to be tainted and thus 'bastard' babies, commanding far less than the infants who had been birthed through the 'purity' of implantation and fertility treatments. Bastard *bambinos* not only lacked the physical and mental attributes of a strong gene pool, but were a health gamble, and took longer to sell.

Whereas a white male infant birthed through the process of implantation or fertility commanded $180,000 U.S., and a white female commanded upwards of $200,000, babies birthed as bastards commanded the paltry sum of $100,000, which greatly displeased the *traficante de reys*, and operation ringleaders. The *jovencitas* who found themselves caught within this undesirable stage of the operation would be found desperately begging for multiple drugs. It was a highly tragic and despicable industry, one which demoralized and demeaned the many women forced to work it, but one that paid well for *traficantes* like Eduardo, and one that paid better yet for the *turistas* and the *traficante de reys* that scoured the city's streets from Europe and the Americas.

If the implantation was successful, the *chica* was considered to be highly valuable and fertile, a true *bebe fabricante,* and two short weeks after the birth was wheeled back to the 'clinic' to be implanted with multiple embryos, expected to birth multiple infants annually until she was sold. The *jovencitas* were bred until their bodies gave out, or after 10 years, whichever transpired first, after which they were sold to the highest bidder, to live out the remainder of their lives as housekeepers and slaves to the wealthy European and African *senoritas* who frequented and shopped the streets of *Lungsod ng Angeles*. The 'lucky' *jovencitas* were those who were sold and who lived to tell the tale, the ones who didn't, bodies now barren and brittle from too many years of abuse bearing too many *bambinos* for the *traficantes*, usually died from self-injected pharmaceuticals of the same variety given them to ensure their compliancy throughout the duration of their pregnancies to the countless *turistas* they had serviced.

Lissy, like the other *jovencitas* who were targeted from the Americas and elsewhere throughout the globe, had been selected for service when she was just a child, her family history gene pool carefully scrutinized, and her addiction to methamphetamine not accidental, nor the tragic poisoning and death of Trevor, both which were orchestrated to assure her compliancy and arrival. An addicted and compliant *jovencita* was a *bebe fabricante* or 'baby-maker' who would withstand the conditioning and birthing process well, a *chica* who would service her men with a smile, selected not only for her addiction and gene pool, but for her stamina as well.

As the night crept over the abandoned library, Lissy fought desperately to work the tape off.

– – –

The little clinic that awaited Lissy's arrival and those of the unfortunate *bebe fabricantes* to come, stood at the center of the city on Atherton Street on a little slope, between a drugstore and a cigar shop, the former serving as provider of the narcotics that the *traficantes,* masquerading as doctors, pumped into the unwilling young women three or four times daily, according to tolerance. Today was Friday, a good day for deliveries because of the increase of traffic upon the city streets, which meant that a *jovencita* could be brought in safely and without notice of arrival. Because of its reputation of providing services to the cities destitute, the clinic was an unlikely suspect of any illegal operation, but every now and then, and if someone was considered to be an informant, they would be killed or paid off by the *traficante de reys*. For the most part, with the exception of an annual inspection for the continuation of its business license, the clinic ran smoothly, and although there was the occasional 'watcher' from the National Labor Organization and the International Collaborative of Health Services for Women, the clinic's 'physicians' maintained a composed front and handled it well. Business was good in brothels like the *Lungsod ng Angeles*, and the city's 'clinic' served its patrons well.

As the day wound down, the *traficante* paced nervously in the clinic's back room, the one that served as exam room and birthing center for the incoming *jovencitas*, and as the supply center for the clinic's surgical equipment and pharmaceuticals, necessities for making the women compliant and calming them down. A frightened or unwilling *chica* was capable of screaming loud and long, behavior which could be heard down the block and which was entirely unacceptable, considering the clinic's central location and illegal operation. A drugged *jovencita* would not only be compliant but lethargic and under the *trafico de rey's* spell, and much more willing to endure the pain of pregnancy and labor, along with the mandatory servicing and 'lessons' that her *traficante* provided on how to become pregnant and please a man well. The fourth stage was the final chance for the *chicas* to maintain their valued status as birthing machines at the 'home' and it was critical that they knew which positions and sexual attributes to use. A highly-drugged *jovencita* was a compliant *jovencita*, one capable of satisfying her *turistas*, *turistas* whose sperm would journey fast and strong up through the birth canal, resulting in the desired *bambino*. While the operation was centered on sex it was a business of money, and the *chicas*, although they were forced into a life of hell, were nourished, fed and clothed. In the city of Makita and others like it, where violence and murder was increasing by the day, it was almost better to be a *jovencita* than a woman of the streets who had to scrounge and beg for her meals.

Thinking of the clinic's upcoming new arrival and of the implantation to result, the *traficante* paced nervously, sterilizing the equipment that would be used for the incoming exam and following procedure in the shabby room. The fact that is was Friday meant that he was one day closer to receiving the girl. His lone wish was for a birth to result, that of a healthy *bambino*, preferably a girl, one birthed nine months and three weeks to the day after the *jovencita's* arrival at the little clinic on the hill.   Wheeled in blindfolded and bound to the dim room and fully drugged before their water broke, the *chicas* were angels, one and all, never knowing what hit them, and losing all memory of the birth at all. Two weeks to the day after giving birth and sometimes sooner, once their uterus had resumed normal position and healed, and whether single or multiple, vaginal or caesarian, they were back in the business of making babies for sale, a position that they now performed both compliant and well.

It was a highly-strategic and lucrative business, one which put the *traficantes* in the delivery room on a high that wouldn't let go, especially when the *bebe fabricantes* were implanted with multiple embryos. The high probability that a multiple birth would result was celebrated like Christmas in the room.

Bahay ng Biyaya

With 600,000 Americans visiting the Philippines each year, 300,000 which permanently stay, and with Australia following the lead, the modest nation was a prime mecca for the baby-making trade. Not only were the *turistas* plentiful, but it was the perfect halfway point for transporting the *jovencitas* from the Americas to Angeles City, then later overseas, for their final duties as housekeepers and slaves to the wealthy. In the third world nation, in addition to tourism a plenty, the drugs ran free, which made the pharmaceuticals that the girls received cost effective to make.

The *Bahay ng Biyaya*, or 'House of Grace' as it was christened by the *traficante de re*ys, a deteriorating structure of stucco and rodent-infested wooden beams, was 'home' to two dozen *jovencitas* of the Philippine sex and baby-making trade the summer that Lissy ran away. On the outskirts of Angeles City and thirty miles northwest of Manila, it lay east of the airport and seven miles west of the city center down a dirt road street. Constructed in 1927, it was comprised of two floors and seven makeshift, dingy rooms, each occupied by several *chicas* in varying stages of 'conditioning,' 'training,' pregnancy, and early labor. When it was determined that a *bebe frabicante* or *jovencita* was ready to birth, she would be whisked off to the clinic and labor would be induced, as a *jovencita* in the pre-labor phase took her place. Whenever the population within the house decreased to below 24, the master of the house would begin preparations for the newest *bebe fabricantes,* who, upon arrival, would be expected to fulfill her new duties with enthusiasm upon her arrival at the House of Grace.

When a *turista* entered the hovel, and only upon either the presentation of the appropriate papers and interrogation, he was escorted without ado to the 'servicing' room, a 10 foot by 10 foot room set aside for the third stage of the operation, sparsely furnished and illuminated by a single candle. From there he would be provided the appropriate, preselected *jovencita*, who would enter the room and recline upon a makeshift bamboo cot upon the dirt floor in the corner. A sheet served as a partition between the other stage 3 girls, at the same time both quieting and concealing them. Forced to remain silent during 'servicing,' they sat upon the dirt waiting for their number to be called. The humiliating rooms had no windows, and when the business at hand was finished, the *turista* would leave and another would take his place, with no break for the girls. The scenario was one of 24 hours, and when a *jovencita* had completed the day's business, she was allowed to sleep for two hours, a time which would find the *bebe fabricantes* crying, praying that they were with child. The *chicas* who were unable to sleep pleaded for extra 'medication' between *turistas,* as they sat upon the dirt behind the sheet with the waiting girls. The third stage was the pinnacle of the *jovencitas* pitiful existence, one to be avoided if at all possible. Many girls, in lieu of sleeping, along with increases in their medication, could be found in the 'training' room.

In all stages of the operation, the *bebe fabricantes* were forced into the brothel's kitchens and fields, cultivating the soil and preparing the next day's meals of rice, *sisig-* a mixture of chopped meat, vinegar, and peppers, and coconut water. There were no toilets, air conditioning, or electrical fans in the *Bahay ng Biyaya*, and life for a *bebe fabricante* was far from easy or normal. Although the Catholic church of *Aming Lady ng Anghel* or 'Our Lady of Angels' lay just down the road, the *jovencitas* weren't allowed to leave the brothel, bound at the ankles by a length of chain that was removed for penetration, and which prevented them from trying to break free from their captors and leaving the brothel. For the *jovencitas* who were not yet pregnant, a normal day was one which was spent traversing from cot to field, and then back again to collapse on the dirt behind the sheet that served as a wall between the rooms. There were no games or books, no snacks between meals, as the *bebe fabricantes* were expected to prepare themselves physically and mentally for the next session. The *chicas* who were 'lucky' enough to be with child, in all stages of pregnancy, were sent for a day of toil in the fields.

The *chicas* meager portions of *sisig* were coated in a mixture of flour, fat, and minerals, and after the meal they were provided with an assortment of mind-numbing pharmaceuticals to take the place of the methamphetamine, alcohol, and heroin. Clothed in thin, soiled robes, they had no toiletries, towels, or blankets. Any luxury was near unheard of, but the wily *jovencita,* in the process of stage 3 servicing, could negotiate with her *turistas* for sweets, cigarettes, toiletries, or other luxuries. Even if the *bebe fabricantes* wanted to, escape from the baneful existence was slim, in the history of the *Bahay ng Biyaya,* not one escape had been successful, and for those who tried to escape their obligations, the end wasn't pretty. Doused in a thick coat of oil, they were either shot or carted off naked and chained, deposited at the bottom of a ravine near the fields.

The summer sun and heavy skies of the brothels were cruel, but winter was the season most feared, for while the ever-present humidity drenched the girls, the drafts and biting cold gave them pneumonia. During the winter, many an ill girl could be seen vomiting on the dirt carpet, and the *jovencitas* who showed this lack of control and respect for their masters did without water at meals. If a *chica* became so ill that she lost consciousness and couldn't service her *turista*, she would be taken to the clinic for evaluation and possible treatment. It was a 'luxury' that didn't happen often, as the penalty for going to the clinic before the induction of labor was three days of solitary confinement without food or water on the roof of the 'home,' in an indoor pen exposed to the elements. The back room in the brothel was reserved for the house's 2 *traficantes* and masters- complete with portable fans, mattresses, and blankets.

It was a rough life once a *jovencita* began producing babies, but life could have been rougher- the *chicas* were thankful that they weren't confined in one of the city's inner brothels. Here, there was no birthing for money and the *turistas* ran wild, with the *chicas* in residence forced to service up to several dozen men a night, a number unheard of in the *Bahay ng Biyaya*. There was no 'training' or luxuries for these girls, no trinkets or scented candles at holiday, not even a ribboned fern or a spoiled morsel of *sisig*- a treat reserved only for the masters of the brothels. If a *jovencita* looked at her imprisonment at the 'home' this way, then existence at the *Bahay ng Biyaya* wasn't so bad after all. Though gone was the life that she had lived in Europe or the Americas, in the land of humidity and mosquito netting the drugs ran a plenty, side dishes which were given freely each day until the *chica* birthed the child.

The 'downside' for the girls was that the final two weeks of pregnancy were the worst of all, for in addition to servicing a greater number of *turistas* and working in the kitchen and fields, the *jovencitas* were forced to withdraw from all pharmaceuticals and drugs, for in order for the *bambinos* to be sold, it was imperative that they were born without disease, and not addicted. It was an efficient, multi-faceted machine; the baby-making business, the *Lupang Hinirang* or 'Beloved Land' that was the Philippines known only in the *jovencitas* dreams. For many of the girls, especially the tender-spirited ones, death or insanity was their only hope.

– – –

In Makita City, one of the sixteen cities that made up the capital of *Manila*, a weary man in casual attire sat hunched over a computer on the 27th floor, staring at the screen. Eyes bleary but wary, he remained fixated on the images before him as one of two hidden cameras revealed another chapter in the saga of the nation's largest sex ring since the days of the old Clark Air Force Base. What he saw was troubling, but provided him with more ammunition for his case, as a foreign man of Spanish descent, dressed in physician's garb and pushing a heavy cart laden with packages, left the drugstore next to the clinic of *Bahay ng Biyaya* to enter the latter's door. Zeroing in on his target, the man whose name was Tha Phah made a few quick adjustments, snapping a close-up of the action, following the 'physician' from the waiting area of the 'clinic' into the first room, where, with a rapid handshake, he delivered his packages. Before he could snap another close-up, the man was out the door and walking quickly upon the street again, leaving the empty cart in the clinic behind him. Studying the footage, Tha Phah smiled. It wasn't enough to bring the case to trial, but it was a start. Lighting a cigar, he remained focused on the footage.

It wasn't out of the ordinary or surprising that the little clinic would purchase its *parmasyutikos* locally, which made it convenient, but it was surprising in regards to what had been purchased, as the clinic's business license was for that of a facility for impoverished women of the region without health insurance, not one licensed to birth the city's babies. In the image that Tha Phah had frozen, carton after carton of Pitocin, a labor-inducing synthetic, signified its presence by a telltale sticker on the sides of the cartons in view of the camera. Tha

Phah, as part of the highly-monitored surveillance conducted since before the beginning of the summer, knew that the clinic did not possess a labor and delivery or birthing license, and had not been authorized for one, only the standard license for practice by a single nurse practitioner or physician, and certainly one that did not allow the writing of labor-inducing and/or heavily guarded narcotics.

Today, like every other day over the course of the summer, Tha Phah kept track of the comings and goings and the daily activity of all those who entered the clinic; surveillance which had begun on the tip of an individual who, while picking up some cough medicine at the adjacent drugstore, had been witness to the muffled screams of someone within. While at the beginning of his surveillance, Tha Phah had not suspected foul play or the unlawful activity of birthing babies for profit, now it was becoming a real possibility. Angeles City was known as *the* prime destination and stop-over for Australian *turistas* and Americans, and it was also the leading city of sex for money, especially with underage children. While Filipino and other local women could easily sell their infants and were the targets of many unsavory men and *traficante de reys*, the offspring of the fresh, white *chica* commanded an immense sum of money, especially the offspring of the *chica* from the Americas. The only 'business' with a comparable profit was that of the selling of illegal drugs like cocaine, heroin, and marijuana.

What Tha Phah had uncovered since April and over the course of the summer had proved enlightening- and what appeared to be an elaborately concealed and clever sex ring, one which targeted white *jovencitas* for the purity of their genes, and for their addiction and birthing capabilities, *jovencitas* who, over the course of the months that he had spent in surveillance, had changed appearance and shape in the stomach. Even more interesting, and what had led to his deduction that the sex ring was operating as a *bebe frabricante* industry, was that 9 days prior he had witnessed and caught on film a girl being wheeled into the clinic one afternoon, and not wheeled out for another twenty four hours, a large, unmarked carton wheeled out behind her.

The captured images sent a shiver through Tha Phah's step, and would assist in bringing down the leaders of the operation; backed by enough evidence he would be set to raid and prosecute the facility that was in illegal operation. He was, in effect, doing what the *traficantes* called '*esperan el momento oportuno,*' or 'waiting for the moment.' When the evidence was full and ripe, his forces would descend in, accompanied by their AK47's and the support of the nation's government. The task of keeping watch over the *Lungsod's dg Angeles*' 'finest' was a daunting one, but one which would reap the cities of Manila and the nation itself much reward. His job was to descend on the den of debauchery and shut down the operation; it was another job entirely to rehabilitate the women, due to the physical and mental abuse they had realized in the hands of the *traficantes*, and countless *turistas*, or men.

Going over the film for the umpteenth time that day, and lighting up another cigar, Tha Phah was both repulsed and prepared. Picking up the phone he dialed out for soup and noodles and poured a glass of whiskey, drinking and smoking until the shivers went away.

8400 miles and 13 hours to the west by direct flight on Asia Air, alongside the east bank of the Sabine River in Louisiana, approximately a half-mile past the iron bridge and directly behind the Veteran's Memorial, in the restroom of the abandoned library that was off the beaten path and now ignored, as Eduardo rounded the curve, Lissy continued her struggle with the tape.

Library

As Eduardo drove, eager for the money, his thoughts roamed as he sang loud and out of tune, tapping weathered, dirty fingernails to the Spanish music on the radio. This time around, with the money that he earned for the safe delivery of the girl into Makita City, and since he had already purchased the heater which would keep his family from freezing in the harsh, Juarez cold, he would purchase his precious Sueso a new dress or two, ones which would make her look like an angel all dolled up for her daddy. And he would buy his wife the expensive and delicate music box that she had always wanted, the one that he thought was hideous- the one with the red cardinal perched on a sprig of sycamore within a thick, glass globe that snowed. He had always detested any sort of contraption that made music, but his Lydia, well; she deserved it for putting up with his travels away from home.

The dress that his Sueso had set her sights on hung in the window of a tiny, non-descript shop in the nearby town of Nogales and was as green as the greenest emerald, with a trim of pale pink ribbons, lace, and bows, because she was such a girly girl, and because she adored receiving something new to wear from her daddy for a present. Eduardo took the greatest pride and care in buying his Sueso such pretty clothes; she was such a good little girl, and he missed her so. He could only hope that the dress shop would still carry the dress that his Sueso had fancied that had been in the window. If not, he would scour the streets of Nogales until he found a dress just like it.

After the gifts were purchased and hidden away in the van, he was going to make a trip home to personally deliver them, because firstly, it was his precious Sueso's birthday in a few days, and second, because it had just been too long since he had been away. Leaning back in the seat and relaxing to the radio, he pictured his Lydia, her raven hair fastened high upon her head and her long neck adorned with pearls, in preparation of their only child's third birthday, mixing a cake and punching down homemade tortillas to bake into enchiladas in the oven. His Lydia would be ecstatic to see him, and his Sueso... oh, how her face would light up like a new Spanish moon all aglow. Thoughts of his cherished family greatly eased his mind as he removed a marijuana cigarette from the glove box, pulling the Chevy off the road at the Veteran's Memorial to enjoy the smoke. It was a good world, a world which would be complete when he was back in the arms of his beautiful Lydia and Sueso, even with all the senseless violence. This would be his last delivery- for awhile.

Relaxing for the first time in weeks, he closed his eyes and smoked. In just a few more minutes, he would have his hands on the *Bahay ng Biyaya's* newest girl, the excitement of the journey fully upon him. Five more minutes after that and she would be hog-tied in the back of his van en route to the airport and to her new life as a *bebe frabricante* for the *turistas*, after he doused her in water. Three to four hours later, God willing, he would arrive with her in tow at the small landing strip that served as an airport several hundred miles northwest of the library and Logansport, where he would deliver her to the waiting *traficante*. From there she would be re-medicated and flown under careful and private surveillance to Makita City, and upon safe arrival, his money would be wired into an account, and he would finally be free to spend it as he pleased, one step closer to home, and to his Sueso.

Picturing this latest scenario, he smiled. He enjoyed the part where, if necessary for compliance, that he would bribe the *jovencitas* with a little something sweet that he had purchased special for the occasion from his hometown of Ciudad, in an effort to ease their minds just a little, after which he would slip in the needle. For this newest *bebe fabricante*, he had brought along some ginger candy, a favorite of his Sueso's, which was why he knew that this newest *chica* would like it. Because it was chewy as all get out, and stuck to the roof of the mouth, he would give her some water, letting her suck upon the rag from the jug, and then, God willing, they would be off on the final leg of his assignment. No hanky-panky and no funny business for this *traficante*, because he had a wife and young daughter at home- just the safe delivery of another frightened and drugged *jovencita*, for whom he had been provided a little box filled with several syringes of the finest methamphetamine that money could buy to make her journey even more comfortable. The *traficante de reys* really knew their stuff.

The *bebe frabricante*, after the series of injections that she received before her arrival in Makita City to the *traficante* who would become her new master, would be drowsy and pliable, already dependent upon what they were giving her, and would have a difficult time recalling anything prior to her capture. He took a final drag of the marijuana and thought about his own little girl, that fuzzy feeling washing over him, and of the dangers of living in Juarez, and the killings in the streets that were coming closer to where they lived, and how he had promised his Lydia that one day he would get them safely out of there.

His old lady had a couple of cousins in Idaho, and God willing, he was going to take her to visit that branch of the family so that his Sueso would know her mother's roots, just as soon as they were settled in to their new life in Jalisco. He was determined to make this delivery his last, and to bid farewell to the *traficante de reys*. He had skills, this *traficante*; prior to signing on as a transporter of human cargo, he had worked at a leather factory in Juarez, and before that he had worked in construction. Ah, Jalisco! It would be a safe and decent community to raise his *precioso* Sueso in. There were far less drug-related killings there, and although the *policia* roamed the streets, they weren't as corrupt as the ones in Ciudad Juarez.

His Lydia, bless her Catholic, God-fearing soul, had been hinting for the longest time how she had wanted to pitch in and help by taking on a paying job to meet the needs of their growing family, and the new city would serve her needs well. She could waitress, a position she had held when they had first met at a road stop in El Paso when he was fresh out of high school. They had their plans, they did, and some darn fine ones at that, and things were not only going to work out, but work out well. He would tackle later the 'minor' but very real problem that the head *hombres* behind the operation's curtain were not in favor of any *traficante,* no matter what the reason, leaving the duties that had been assigned them, the very reason that he had been hired for his position in the first place was because he had a family.

Clearing this uneasy thought from his mind and sucking down the last of the cigarette, he revved up the engine and turned in the direction of the library, inhaling the marijuana's sweet smoke. Time and daylight was wasting, and he had no idea how long this *jovencita* had been laying there gagged and waiting, the horror that one day he would find one of them dead always on his mind. The air inside the cab had cooled to a pleasant 89 degrees, even with all his worry, which meant that this *chica* would most certainly make it. By the time he reached the library, he had calmed his fears again, ready to just enjoy the ride with this newest *bebe fabricante.* He only wished that he could have sex with her, like the other *traficantes* did regardless of their marital status, but it was out of the question, as he was a faithful *traficante* to his wife and family, something he took great pride in.

He had heard that there were many *turistas* waiting to sire a baby with one of the girls, hundreds, possibly even thousands, in the hopes of being one of the lucky ones selected from the gene pool. Although he had never caught a glimpse of one of them, he had heard that they were screened even more than the *jovencitas* themselves, passing extensive background checks, physicals and blood work with flying colors. Wishing that he was in possession of such marvelous genes that were capable of fathering a white *jovencita's* child, he turned off the engine. What a grand life he could lead as a *turista* and sire to one of these *chicas*, ah yes, indeed. The thought was incomparable.

At some point in his life, he would have to stop being fearful of the ringleaders who ran the operation and pleasured out the *bebe frabricantes* for money; if he was ever to be a real father to his Sueso, he would have to stand up on his own two feet and set a good example. What if he and Lydia wanted to make a new baby of their own, possibly another *precioso* little girl? No matter how hard he tried to psyche himself up for each delivery with a clear mind, the more he realized that he needed a break. He had been working too long and hard in the dirty game, and had been happier and more at peace when life was simple, and when he was working in the factory. Nowadays, each time that he woke just a little bit farther away from home, uneasy thoughts would jar his brain, and at night when he called it a day, he would contemplate how long it would take for one of the kingpins behind the curtain to flesh him out and put a blade to his face, because they were just plain tired of him or they didn't approve of how he ran his side of the operation, or because a *jovencita*, bless her pitiful soul, had died along the way. Walking into the abandoned library, Eduardo followed the directions he had been provided with, en route to the restroom. As he opened the door to the stall, the young *chica* upon the floor let out a muffled scream.

"*Jovencita*, have no fear," he whispered, walking toward her calmly, and guiding the needle into a vein. "There's more where this came from, and you're going to be okay."

Smoothing back the safflower hair from her face and kissing his finger and placing it to her forehead, Eduardo dragged Lissy into a sitting position as she struggled to get away. Feeling the drug's glorious effects on her body and desperate for the calm that it provided her, she slipped into sleep. No ginger candy or necessary for this *bebe fabricante*, the Mexican stroked her face.

"There, there, my *precioso jovencita*," he bade her. "*Eres una cosa bonita*." "You're a pretty thing."

172

Carrying the sleeping girl out of the library and into the back of the waiting van, he took great care into dousing her with a jug of water and placing her into the waiting burlap bag, positioning it just so among the sacks of grain. Placing a call to announce the time of his arrival, he jammed the van into high speed, heading off to the airstrip that served as Freeman Airport three hundred and twenty two miles northwest of Logansport away. Satisfied with the girl's condition and complacency, and in early celebration of the ease of this delivery, he lit up another joint and directed a satisfied glance Lissy's way.

"*Santo Dios, la Madre Maria, tenga mucho cuidado de que,*" the Mexican whispered. "May God's holy mother Mary take good care of you on your way."

- - -

173

Encased in the burlap and drifting in and out of sleep, Lissy fought to breathe. Not quite an hour into her journey, the air in the sack was already almost nonexistent in the tight space. Tied behind her, her hands hurt, and her mouth and feet, still wrapped in tape, felt the same. Fighting off the panic that was overtaking her, she tried to work herself free, but the injection had served its purpose, and she was too sleepy and weak. The only sounds that she could hear was the bump-bumping of the truck as the wheels made contact with the road, and the Mexican humming to music. As she listened to his off-beat singing, everything that her mother and Steven had ever told her about her chosen lifestyle all came flooding in- the dangers of taking drugs, of hanging with the wrong crowd, and how anything could happen to anyone who was involved in any way. And Trevor, poor, poor boy. It was her fault that he was dead. The tears came, welling up against the tape, as the Mexican continued to sing.

As the van bumped along down the road en route to the airstrip, she tried to stay awake enough to think. The last thing that she remembered was drinking beer on Bourbon Street. From there, her thoughts took her to the burlap sack and to the duct tape around her face, and to the ethereal feel of the meth that had been injected into her veins.

It was the drugs, it had to be. Her mother and Steven had been right, Trevor had been right; they should have never become involved- never taken the trip across the border to score some meth- nothing. They should have played it safe. But now, it was too late. Trevor was dead, and she was well on her way.

Wondering what the Mexican had in store for her, Lissy moaned, her voice echoing meekly through the tape, and just loud enough for Eduardo to hear, as he stopped the van just long enough to guide another needle into her skin, which made her mind feel good again, and her worries go away. Her breath becoming shallow, she struggled to breathe. Untying the burlap and dousing her with another jug of water, the Mexican's thoughts ran again to his *precioso* Sueso, and to the joys of this final delivery, then to the new life that he was going to provide for his family. With any luck, he would have enough money left to buy the gas necessary to drive the family up to Idaho, at least for a little while.

His Lydia had kept a letter that one of her cousins had written her, one which told about the ponies that ran free across the fields, and the night sky that was so full of stars that they just shot across the sky. The letter had made him yearn to see the land of wild ponies and shooting stars for himself, and for his Sueso, and if it was the last thing he did, after he relocated his family, he would get them all up there one day. He wished no ill luck upon this newest *jovencita*, if it was up to him, which it wasn't, she would ride with him in the front of the van, where they would have sex and sip whiskey and chew ginger candy, but he had been ordered otherwise, as the likelihood of someone seeing them and getting a whiff of his business with this newest *chica* just too great. The *policia* patrolled the Louisiana roads with diligence, even the roads off the highway. There was no escape anywhere from the police.

"There, there, my pretty, there, there," he whispered as Lissy faded away. *"Estamos a una hora de Freeman."* "We're an hour from Freeman."

Avoiding the puddle of mud in the road, he crossed the state line into Mississippi, pushing the pedal to the floorboard just as far as it would go. The humid air was now heavy with mosquitoes and he was tired. No longer did he want to give this *jovencita* any sex or candy, he just wanted to finish the job. Besides, if she was pregnant upon arrival, the *traficante de reys* would be quick to slice his throat, and the throats of his *precioso* Lydia and Sueso.

His money and the narrow landing strip that masqueraded as an airport a mere ten miles down the muddy road, the Mexican whistled, rubbing the soiled rag madly to his face and pressing the van on as white smoke billowed out from the tailpipe of the worn truck. The airport had been selected for its out-of-the-way location within the Mississippi hills, and for the availability of the private plane that would be waiting. Exasperated at the mud that had accumulated on the road, and swatting another mosquito, Eduardo punched the steering wheel. Lissy woke to hear the Mexican swearing and the van screech to a stop, as Eduardo got out and dug a shovel into the ground.

"Santa Maria Madre, ten piedad! No puedo illegar tarde!" "Holy Mother Mary, have mercy! I can't be late!"

As the Mexican fervently prayed the Holy Mother's name between obscenities, the van remained stuck in the mud, front wheels frozen, as he continued to shovel away.

One thing was certain; if he was late to meet the plane it would cost him a hefty chunk of his money.

Over the next hill, beside the waiting plane, the Filipino *traficante* in the dark starched suit consulted his watch again, spitting upon the dial.

— — —

In the makeshift room that served as the family kitchen in a plywood shack on the outskirts of Ciudad, Juarez, adorned in curlers atop a halo of coal, a woman kneaded biscuits for Sunday breakfast as a child danced round. Pausing to kiss the eager toddler, she resumed chopping a ripened mango to add to the bowl. There had been gunfire last night somewhere close to their humble abode, after which she had been unable to return to sleep. Although the gunfire was nothing new, remaining somewhere off in the distance, it was slowly migrating towards them and away from the city. The child christened Sueso had slept peacefully through, her mamma stroking her dark curls.

In this city of 2.5 million people, over 15,000 misfortunate souls had lost their lives last year, a statistic which Eduardo's wife Lydia, a pious woman who had attended Catholic services every Sunday for 35 years until the escalating violence of the drug wars, kept track of faithfully. If the figure was anywhere near correct, as the newspapers claimed it to be, that was nearly 40 people every 24 hours dying here, many of them innocents caught within the crossfire. The majority of the deaths were due to the escalading drug wars between rival cartels, wars which saw an increase in violence in the winter of 2006, when President Manuel Gomez initiated the involvement of federal troops to the state troops already fighting the war. She had heard how the guerrillas, posing as soldiers, would come in the night and take young men from their homes for the cause. The ill-fated boys had two choices, to join the cartels, or to die by a bullet to the skull. It was a dangerous time to be living in; made worse by her husband's missing presence from the home. Whereas she missed him greatly and prayed constantly for his safety, his *precioso* Sueso missed him even more. Nervously whispering a prayer, Lydia paused again to let the little girl lick the spoon. It was a good thing that she had born a girl.

Making her uneasiness worse was the raid that had been conducted on a private residence in Tamaulipas, Mexico a week ago, one which had led to the confiscation of over 300 million U.S. dollars in marijuana, adding to the retaliation and anger of the nightly gunfire, as Lydia faced the nearby violence alone. Night after night she would cover her head with a pillow, whispering 'Ave Marie' over and over again for only the Holy Mother to hear. While she was saddened over the lack of her husband's presence, she knew that his disappearance was necessary if they were ever to leave Juarez to relocate in Jalisco. Since his departure, he had kept the details of his new employment secret, saying only how he had been fortunate to have secured a position in transportation, a job not only stable, but high-paying as well.

What more could she really have asked for? She was thankful for her family, and for their meager home.

To have landed a job, much less to have found one that paid well, was an almost unheard of occurrence in the densely-populated border town, as the only employment was within the *maquiladoras* and *maquilas* or assembly plants and factories, and within the hush-hush world of the state and federal forces who kept tainted control over the drug lords and kingpins within the cities 15 townships. Thinking of how a full 50% of the city's businesses had shut their doors, and of the 400,000 people who had fled the *Chihuahuan* desert city, Lydia nervously grabbed a stool. While she was doubtful of her husband's sincerity because it sounded just too good to be true, she wanted desperately to believe him. Climbing upon a stool, she lifted a small box out from behind a piece of wood as the little girl playing with the hem of her skirt gave it an impatient pull.

"*Parada, Sueso! Dejar ir! O no Habra galletas en el desayuno pera comer!*" "Stop, *Sueso*! Let go! Or there will be no biscuits to eat at breakfast!"

Ignoring her momma to give the dress another pull, the little girl who was the pride of Eduardo's life and dreams stuck a chubby finger in her mouth and toddled towards the bowl. Giving her *mama* a coy smile, she plunged her fingers in.

"*Sueso!*"

Lydia's tone towards the baby girl turned sharp, as there was no time for nonsense this morning, for there were clothes to scrub in the bucket that served as a tub, and potatoes to peel for the evening meal. Giving the child a light slap on the hand, she resumed counting the money, her forehead wrinkling into a frown. While upon last count there had been 10 cellophane-wrapped stacks of one thousand dollar bills, today there were only nine. Either she was too tired to keep an accurate count, or something was desperately wrong. The money in the box was their life savings, money which came from her husband's new job, the down payment for their new home; savings they had been able to accumulate since the violence in Juarez had escalated and had become increasingly close. It was a mistake in counting, that was all. There had always been 9 wrapped stacks of bills in the box.

No one knew where she hid the money, not even Eduardo. The lack of sleep was taking its toll.

Carefully returning the box to its hiding place behind the wood, Lydia climbed down from the stool to place the biscuits on the stovetop to cook and let Sueso lick the bowl. Squealing in delight, the child stuck her fingers into the batter and slid a chubby finger into her mouth. It was going to be a good Sunday, the Sunday before Sueso turned three years old. And one day soon, their beloved Eduardo was coming home.

My dearest Lissy,

It's been 15 days now and still no word. I went ahead and attended Back to School night last night to try to get my head out of this whirl, but it wasn't the same without you. This week has been really rough, signing you up for classes without knowing what you want to take your junior year was especially rough, but I was told that if they aren't what you wanted to take, that you can always change them when you get home. At first, I was going to lie and tell everyone that asked that you were visiting family out of town, and then I thought better of it and told the truth because eventually, the truth will come out.

But what is the truth? That you will be home any day now. And that, my darling daughter, is all that counts.

It's 3 am and I can't sleep right now, but that isn't unusual. Just like every night since you've been gone, no matter what the time, I'm still up.

Lissy, are you up, too? Are you having trouble sleeping, my beautiful daughter, because you feel guilty about not calling us yet or coming home? If you are, let me tell you a little something that might help.

When I was little and had trouble falling asleep, my mother would tell me what her mother, your great-grandmother, told her, and that I am now telling you. Your great-grandmother was a kind-hearted, good woman and she was also very poor, just like many people of those days. She lived in Mallow, Wales with her mother, your great-great-grandmother in a little house and who, in the evenings, would cook her a supper of crawdads and venison upon the stove.

One day, when she was just a young girl, she got up at dawn like she always did to walk down to the creek that runs from Mallow to Cork, where she would pan for moon dust until her mother, your great-great grandmother, called her in to supper with a kettledrum. She was panning for moon dust because her mother, your great-great-grandmother had told her that even the smallest sprinkle would make the most tired person in the world fall asleep. Now on this particular day, there was a hint of sunshine in the sky, which was highly unusual for Mallow, because the sun never shined. So, your great-grandmother already knew that this day was going to be very special, which is why when she went out that morning to pan for the elusive dust that would help her sleep, she took along a little bag. Just a small one, in case she really did find moon dust in that creek.

Well, it got to be late in the afternoon and your great-grandmother had been panning and panning and still no moon dust, not even a hint of a sprinkle, and she was very tired because she hadn't slept in days, but since she had never found any moon dust yet, she kept on trying. And the sun was shining so bright that every time she looked at it, it burned her eyes. She was weary, and hungry, too, and it took all her strength just to swish the pan back and forth in the creek, back and forth, back and forth, in her quest for the most elusive dust in the world. When she was so tired that she could barely stand, she looked at the sun again, except this time it burned her eyes so bad that she had to rub them to make them stop hurting, but that didn't work so she rubbed them again but they still hurt so she dipped her hands in the creek and rinsed her face with water and when she looked up she saw a mother deer standing there. Well, your great-grandmother, since she was so hungry, wanted to take the deer back home so that her mother could cook it for them to eat, since she hadn't found any moon dust anyway.

"What business do you have here at my creek?" the deer said to your great-grandmother, swishing her speckled tail gently to and fro as she bent her graceful neck close to your great-grandmother's face.

Well, when your great-grandmother saw that fine doe she wanted it more than anything, even the moon dust that she had come down to find.

"I'm here to find moon dust because I can't sleep," your great-grandmother said. "But instead, I found myself a very fine doe that I'm going to take home with me."

But then your great-grandmother remembered that she didn't have anything to catch the doe with, just the pan and the little bag.

"You must be thirsty, so please, take a drink," your great-grandmother said to the deer, offering her some water from the pan, in hopes that it would get close enough that she could hit it over the head with it.

But the mother deer knew that your great-grandmother only wanted her for the dinner table, so she stayed a safe distance away.

"If you give me that small bag in your hand, I'll fill it with sand from the creek," said the deer. "And at night when you want to sleep, just rub some on your pillow and it will turn into moon dust before your eyes and you will have sweet dreams. But I'll give it to you only on one condition, which is that you must promise that you will never, ever, for as long as you live, kill and eat any deer or creature of the forest again."

Well, your great-grandmother was a pretty smart girl, just like you, and she wasn't about to be fooled by a deer, no matter how gentle or sweet, and besides, it was moon dust that she was after, not sand.

"I don't want your sand, I came here for moon dust," your great-grandmother said as she resumed panning in the creek.

But then she remembered how awfully tired she was, and how she hadn't slept in 10 days, and she knew right then and there that she would have to take the deer up on her offer, or she would die without any sleep. She knew that she had an important decision that she needed to make- to eat the gentle creatures of the forest, or to be able to sleep.

"Alright," said your great-grandmother as she handed the deer the bag. "I'll take your sand, and in exchange for your wisdom and kindness, I will never kill and eat your kind or any of the other creatures of the forest ever again."

So your great-grandmother watched as the deer swirled the little bag round and round in the creek, and when she handed it back to her, it was filled with sand, just like she had said, and not only did your great-grandmother not believe, *but she was suddenly very scared because she didn't believe in talking deer and it was moon dust that she was after, anyway.*

"May your sleep be always restful and your dreams sweet," said the deer with another swish of her tail in your great-grandmother's face. "I must go now. Good day."

Now, your great-grandmother had never seen a talking deer, or heard of anyone who had, and she was just about ready to faint. But she held the small bag of sand tight because she couldn't sleep.

That night, when your great-grandmother arrived home for supper, your great-great grandmother put a plate of venison before her upon the table again, but your great-grandmother didn't eat. She only drank water and went to bed hungry, but she pretended to eat so as not to make her mother feel bad, and hid the uneaten meat beneath her skirt until she left the table. And that night when she went to bed she was so, so tired and so incredibly hungry, but she had kept her word to the mother deer, and was going to abide by it.

Before she lay down, she took the little bag and rubbed just the smallest bit of sand upon her pillow before she laid her head down to sleep. She was more hungry and tired than she had ever been, and mad at herself for not finding any moon dust, but she closed her eyes anyway. As soon as her head hit the pillow, the sand worked its magic and became moon dust that worked its magic and your great-grandmother was fast asleep, dreaming the sweetest, most peaceful dreams that she had ever dreamed. And when she got out of bed in the morning, she was no longer tired but full of life and energy, and not only that but when she walked into the kitchen, it was full of all sorts of fruits and vegetables and other wonderful things to eat.

Your great-grandmother right then and there kept her promise to the deer and never ate venison again, or any other creatures that lived in the forests of Wales, only fruit and vegetables, and there wasn't a night that went by that the cupboards weren't full and that she didn't take a little bit of sand and it turned to moon dust before her very eyes upon her pillow at night, giving her dreams that were soft and sweet, and a peaceful sleep.

To this day, each night before she goes to sleep, your grandmother rubs her pillow with a bit of the sand and it turns to moon dust and she is always able to get to sleep.

Lissy, I'm a little tired now, and I bet that you are, too, so I'm going to close my eyes for a little while. I hope that tonight while I'm sleeping will be the night that you come home because I love and miss my little girl more than you will ever know.

All my love forever,

See you soon-

Mom.

Mississippi

The van continued to remain stuck no matter how many times Eduardo forced the shovel in, the weight of the mud upon the wheels just too great. Wiping the sweat from his forehead, he cursed the mud which had become glue in the Mississippi sun. He was going to pay for this, he just knew it. As the sun sunk in the last light of day and the last of the mosquitoes flew away, he ripped off his shirt, throwing it into the hole that the tires had made, tossing the shovel in after it. He was late and would have to call the *traficante de rey* right away. If there was one golden rule that he had learned over the last three years, it was to deliver his cargo on time, every time, always, no matter what. Nothing else mattered. There were no excuses in the game.

Kicking at a tire in frustration, he fell to the dirt and wept. If he couldn't figure out a way to get himself out of this mess within the next few minutes, this latest *jovencita* would surely suffocate, the air flow in the van nonexistent. He would have to remove her from the back of the van, untie the burlap sack, and douse her with water again, a move that would take critical time away. And there was always the possibility that no matter how much water he doused her with, she would still die in the Mississippi heat.

What if someone saw him untying his sack of human wheat? What if the policia were on their way? What if he was punished severely for this mistake?

As Eduardo threw his head to the sky and howled in fear, Lissy lay listening, drenched in sweat from the lack of any circulating air. The guttural sobbing made her heart race, as she lay in fear for what would happen next. Her only option was to lie still and feign death, leading the Mexican to believe that she already died from the heat. Wrapped from head to toe in burlap and imprisoned by the tape, it was the only choice she could make. The last injection was beginning to wear off and her body was coming to, she could feel it, as she struggled to loosen the tape. With any luck, if he feared her dead, he would forego her next injection. As she fought with the tape, she heard a noise from the vicinity of the tailgate.

He was coming back for her! What if he saw the loose tape?

Calming her mind and holding her breath, she listened as the Mexican approached the van and opened the tailgate as her heart raced. It was all she could do to lay still, and when he opened the sack and saw the lack of color upon her face, he let out a horrific scream that curdled every bone in Lissy's body.

"Madre Maria ten piedad de mi!" "Mother Mary, have mercy on me!"

Terrified that his precious cargo was near death or dead, he peeled off the tape that covered Lissy's nostrils to let in the air, as she fought for her life to hold her breath. Wetting a finger, he placed it beneath her nose for what seemed like a lifetime to her to see if she was breathing, but felt nothing. In the time that it had taken him to try to dig the van out of the mud the temperature inside had climbed to 98 degrees, a critical mistake, much too hot for a *chica* imprisoned in burlap and tape.

How long had he been digging to free the wheels?
Fifteen minutes? An hour?

Checking to make sure that her hands were still tied behind her, and not wanting to waste any more time by checking for a pulse, he doused Lissy with water again, and slapped her face. As he lived and breathed, this was one *jovencita* who would live to make beautiful babies for the Filipino *traficante de reys*.

With a body like that, oh, what beautiful babies she would make. Forgive me, for I have sinned, Holy Mary.

Crossing himself and praying to the Holy Virgin Mary for a miracle, he studied her desperately, an angel in evening wear and burlap, and kissed the pale face. His Lydia had told him that her own mother had witnessed a miracle, and although he had never seen one, he believed. He looked up to the sky, crossing himself fervently, in hopes that his miracle would be achieved. What he didn't notice was that the tape around Lissy's ankles was beginning to give way.

The *bebe frabricante* had been sufficiently cooled and given air, and although there was no visible sign of life, there was hope. He would place the dreaded call, to explain about the mud and how it was making him late, after which he would give the *jovencita* another injection, check for a pulse, and if all was good, he would take whatever punishment was thrown him, and beg for mercy before the wrath of the *traficante*. But if she had no pulse and the injection didn't bring her around, he would have to immediately take another step, mixing another syringe of meth with some adrenalin.

And if that didn't wake the *jovencita* from her 'sleep,' he was doomed.

Falling to his knees and fervently crossing his chest, he placed the call, spilling his guts about the mud, and how the *traficante de rey* would have to come down and pick up the girl, but nothing of the fact that this latest *jovencita* appeared dead.

What difference did an hour or two make? She was as good as at the airport, anyway!

But make a difference it did, and the resulting conversation wasn't good.

One thousand dollars out of his hard-earned money for a late delivery? Why? How could they do this to him? He had mouths to feed, and a family to move out of Juarez! It wasn't fair.

He had followed through on his part of the deal; the *chica* was almost there. It was no sweat off anyone's back, save for leaving the plane unattended for a bit, and it certainly wasn't his fault that the van had become stuck in the wet Mississippi earth. Besides, he had not been informed about the condition of the terrain in the first place. But neither anger nor begging worked, as he tore at his hair and threw the phone into the dirt.

"*Yo soy un idiota.*" "I am an idiot."

And he was also out of water, using up the last of what was in the third and final jug to douse Lissy with.

Why hadn't he doused her with whiskey instead? Ah, he was an idiota, for sure. Not like the other traficantes who pumped their deliveries full of sex and whiskey, to pass the time on the trail. But he was a family man, a good man, a man that his precioso Sueso could be proud of.

Faced with two difficult choices short of putting a gun to his head, Eduardo hung his head and prayed for himself and his family. His first option was to walk to the stream to replenish the jugs before giving the *chica* her next injection, as the sun was going down anyway. The second was that he could sit and wait for the *traficante* to pick her up, in which case the *chica* would most certainly die before he got there. Either way, he had to do something. Deciding on the water and praying for mercy, Eduardo grabbed a jug from the van and headed in the direction of the stream. If the *chica* wasn't alive when the *traficante de rey* got there… well, he preferred not to think about it.

Wrestling with the tape, the last of it coming free from her feet, hands still trapped behind her, Lissy wiggled free from the burlap to roll from the open tailgate into the dirt on her face. Panicking at the thought that the Mexican might have heard, she scanned the surrounding terrain. To her right, and towards the lake, the Mexican was walking away. To her left stood the massive oaks of the Mississippi landscape, and a more level terrain. Wondering if he had a gun and how long it would take for him to discover that she had escaped, she ran in the direction of the trees, impeded by not having her hands free.

Where would she run to? Was there anyone around who could help her? Were there any houses? How far off was the nearest highway or the city? What would the Mexican do with her if he captured her? Would he kill her? What was she worth to save? How would he kill her?

Trying to silence her mind, she had one goal: to make it to the shelter of the trees before the Mexican returned and discovered her missing. If she was able to make it that far, she could make it over the hill, and on to the nearest highway.

There had to be a highway. Or someone, somewhere. Every road leads to a highway.

One step at a time, one foot in front of the other, she struggled to her feet to run for her life. With a last glance behind her, the Mexican nowhere in sight, she ran as fast as her legs would carry her toward the trees.

What if he shot at her? What if he got in the van and then shot at her? Was the madman capable of hitting a target out of range? How far could a bullet travel anyway? How many bullets did he have?

Exhausting herself with questions, she ran without stopping until she reached the safety of a tree as she threw herself behind it, protected by the trunk of the wide old oak tree. Her heart was pounding, and with her arms behind her, she still couldn't breathe.

He had to have reached the lake by now. He had to be on his way back to the van with the water. How long had she been running? Three minutes? Fifteen? Did he know she had escaped?

Afraid to get up and make a move, but even more afraid to stay where she lay, Lissy struggled to her feet, continuing her escape through the trees. As the terrain gave way to a gentle slope, she struggled to keep on running. While running with her hands tied behind her was one thing, running in three inch heels and a cocktail dress was entirely another, as she kicked off her shoes to run in bare feet. Breathing heavily, she paused just long enough to look behind her, and seeing nothing, turned to run again. She was climbing the hill with a newfound speed and had put a good amount of distance between herself and the Mexican. She was going to make it.

– – –

Filling the jugs with water, Eduardo breathed a sigh of relief, beginning the trek back up to the van. The *jovencita* was going to make it, and even though the *traficante de reys* were keeping half of his money over his "mistake," he had just enough in savings to move the family to Jalisco. This was his last delivery, and his Sueso was waiting. He could hardly wait to see her, dressed in ribbons and bows, her chubby hands wrapped in an embrace around his face. When they got to Jalisco he would surprise her with the pony that she had been begging for ever since the circus had come to Juarez almost three summers ago, and she had ridden one round a circle. It had been a good summer that year, full of cotton candy and his Sueso's bubbly laughter, and he had carried the picture of her upon the pony in his pocket ever since, which made him happy. Gazing upon it now, his heart gladdened.

Feeling better and with a bounce in his bootstraps, Eduardo walked faster down through the grass to revive Lissy before the arrival of the *traficante*. The waning sun felt good on his face, and Mississippi, while not as strikingly beautiful as the wild open country of waterfalls and mountains that was Mexico, and for all of its muddy roads, was still pretty darn breathtaking. The tall, soft reeds, the wide oak trees, the catfish floating lazily, the song of the *'cicada'* or locusts as they emerged from the earth after almost two decades into adults, the cool, star-studded sky of the evenings... As he walked, he thought about the mystery of it all, and of his Lydia and his *precioso* Sueso, and how he could hardly wait to see her face light up upon his arrival back home.

It was almost his baby girl's dinnertime in Mexico, and he wondered what Lydia had made for the table. She'd dress it with a red cloth first, one that she had washed in the bucket. His Sueso liked a lot of things, applesauce, corn, tortillas, and tomatoes... everything but squash and green vegetables. And ice-cream, oh, how she loved it so! Strawberry and vanilla, home-spun with caramel upon it.... Just the thought of it made him want some.

Approaching the van, Eduardo rounded the back, yearning for a bowl of ice cream with caramel drizzled upon it, like his Sueso. No doubt, dinner over, she would be slurping it down with a giggle beneath her halo of curls. Lydia, bless her smooth, dark neck of pearls, would never believe, not even when he told her- that he was coming home. No more transporting oranges! He could finally be the husband that the last three years had taken out of him, and a father to his little girl. Feeling like the luckiest man in the world, he saw the length of tape in the dirt. As he stared at in disbelief, the waiting *traficante* appeared from behind the front of the van. A well-dressed Filipino male attired in a business suit and loafers, he was pointing a pistol at Eduardo.

"*La nina, ella esta viva, si?*" "The girl, she is alive, yes?"

Tossing the sacks of wheat about as if they were boxes of ginger candy, desperate to find the *jovencita* within, Eduardo begged for his life.

"*Por favor! Ten piedad de mi! Tengo una familia!*" " Please! Have mercy upon me! I have a family!"

As the bullet exploded in his face, Eduardo thought about his angelic Sueso.

His precioso child. So innocent, so sweet. He would love her for a lifetime, wherever that may be. She was, and would always be, his beautiful Sueso.

Whistling softly, the *traficante de rey* wiped down the pistol. Hearing the gunshot, Lissy looked back down the hill to see one man fall and another coming after her.

— — —

At the marketplace, Lydia bartered for mangos. They looked extra good today, with a thick flesh of mottled green, and smelled sweet.

"*Cuanto?*" "How much?"

With Sueso in tow, she strapped the basket of fruit to her back, eager to begin the journey home to prepare the day's meal.

"*Date prisa, Sueso!*" "Hurry, Sueso!"

The little girl was fussy today, not her usual self, having been up the night before with a stomach ache, no doubt from licking just a little too much of the uncooked batter the day before. Lydia had quietly listened to the gunfire while rocking the baby tightly to her chest, a cool cloth pressed lovingly to her middle, leaving the little girl alone only to draw a little tighter the sheet that served as a barrier between their humble home and all the violence. In a sleep interrupted by nightmares, she had slept with the toddler tight to her chest, the damp cloth still pressed against her middle. Now, urging Sueso on with a gentle push, she finally gave up, lifting her to her bosom with a kiss. The warm summer air was only turning warmer, and her precious baby needed comforting.

"*Ahi, ahi. Mama esta aqui.*" "There, there. Mamma's here."

She was excitedly awaiting Eduardo's arrival, as just yesterday he had phoned to say that he was finally coming home to see them, and had a surprise to tell her. She could only guess what it was that he wanted to tell her, but was hoping that it had something to do with their move to Jalisco.

She, too, could hardly wait to get out of Ciudad, Juarez. She too, had a surprise to tell- that she was pregnant with child, the brief visit that her husband had made last year proof of their growing family. Now, their family would be complete, and she could place another plate upon the table.

The gunfire the evening prior had been close, too close, and with a toddler and another *bambino* on the 'stove,' it was past time to get out. Their Eduardo was coming home in three days, and she had a celebration to get underway and a birthday cake to make with candles for Sueso's third birthday. She had wrestled with whether or not to tell the little girl that her daddy was coming home, because it would overexcite her and make her difficult to handle, but she had told her anyway, and was glad. Sueso had squealed in joy and her face had lit up, as she danced round and round with laughter. That was surely another reason for the little girl's stomach ache- all the excitement. She had taken to talking about her daddy nonstop since she had told her that he was coming home, in time for her birthday even. Holding the little girl a little closer, Lydia thought about the celebration and about all the food that there would be upon the table. As she walked, her mind raced in anticipation.

There was the *albondigas* soup with tortillas, a favorite of Eduardo's, because of the meatballs. And fresh corn and mangoes from the market. And for the grand finale of it all- chocolate cake with real cocoa and strawberry ice-cream. What a celebration they would have, and she was thankful. On top of the world because their Eduardo was coming home, the weight upon her shoulders unnoticeable, Lydia picked up her pace towards the little shack that served as the family home. It was time to prepare for her husband's arrival.

Pulling back the sheet and still holding Sueso, she saw the butt of a cigarette upon the table, which meant only one thing, that her Eduardo was home, and she wouldn't have to wait three more long days after all.

"Alabado sea Jesus y Madre Santa Maria!" "Praise Jesus, and holy Mother Mary!"

"Sus oraciones habian sido contestadas por fin!" "Her prayers had finally been answered!"

Before she could open her mouth and beg for her life and the life of her daughter, Lydia and *Sueso* fell to the floor in a round of gunfire, after which the *sicario* for the *traficante de rey* ransacked the humble shack and fled with the money.

River

Running for her life and darting in and out of the scattered oaks on the hillside, Lissy climbed the slope, wondering how long it would take for the man to find her. The sun had disappeared from the sky and it was almost dark, and the last thing she wanted to do was to run blindly through the night. She would have to hurry. Whoever was following her was armed, and although she didn't want to stop, she was more fearful of moving on, so she would have to find somewhere to wait out the night.

The man had a gun. How far could he fire it? How fast could he run?

Praying like she had never prayed before, Lissy ran until she came to the top of the slope, where, catching her breath, she stared in awe at the wide stretch of river meandering lazily below her. Unbeknown to her, she had come upon the mighty Mississippi, its 2300 miles of water flowing from St. Louis, Missouri, into the Gulf of Mexico. The largest watershed in the United States, it was home to a large variety of plants and wildlife.

A river! Surrounded by trees for as far as she could see! If she could just make it down there before he saw her, she could wait out the night in the forest along its mighty bank.

Exhausted, Lissy ventured a look behind her, scanning the vast prairie and clusters of trees for any sign of life. It was dark, and the man who had killed the Mexican could be hiding, or right beside her, and she would never know it. Facing her fears head-on, she started running, her legs barely able to keep up with her mind. In full view of anything and anyone, she had to make it down to the river, into the protection of the trees that ran alongside it.

She would make it. She would do it for Trevor. His death would not be in vain. She would run alongside the river like she had never run before, within the protection of the forest until she came across someone who could help her. Someone with a phone, so she could call her parents. They would pick her up, and her nightmare would be over.

But unbeknown to her was that it was a 40 minute drive by car to the nearest town, and a 35 mile walk on foot.

As she ran in the dark, she felt sick, her bound arms swelling at the wrists. In withdrawal from the meth, at any time her stomach or her legs would cramp up again, in which case she would have a hard time getting anywhere, especially with her hands behind her back. As she flew to the safety of the river's thick clusters of cottonwoods, she heard the sound of footfall somewhere alongside her in the grass.

There was no one back there. It was her paranoia setting in. She had had a good head start over whoever was following her, and she was determined to keep it.

Reaching the river's edge, she stumbled along the rocks in the dark, running towards the trees in search of cover, and somewhere to wait out the night.

What if he found her? What if, while she was sleeping, he put a bullet to her head? What did he want from her? Where was he planning to take her? Had her parents paid her ransom?

Sobbing uncontrollably in fear and vomiting up the spoiled water, Lissy fell upon the rocks, cutting her wrist, picking herself up to run blindly towards the forest. Her ankles were swollen and bruised from the tape and they hurt almost as much as her arms did, and she desperately needed a fix again. She had never felt so cold, so alone, so dark, so sick. The cocktail dress that she had worn to the bar in the French Quarter was torn and had vomit upon it, and every bone in her body ached and she wanted her mother and father.

Where was her phone when she needed it? Where was the man who was following her? Where was some meth? She needed a pick-me-up and she needed it fast.

The forest before her, Lissy ran until she was tripped by a branch, falling face first onto the cool earth, hitting her head. Whimpering, she lay in pain, then crawled below it, rolling as best she could to try to cover herself with twigs and leaves from the towering cottonwoods. It was pointless, she needed her hands, and she was going to die here.

But she had done it. She had made it to the forest. Whoever was following her would have no idea where she was. Or would he? What was he doing? Was he walking blindly? Running? Was he waiting until daylight to come after her? Was he alone? Had he called for backup to help him?

As the night wore on, Lissy lay quiet in the forest where she had fallen, listening for anything that might signify that the man with the gun had found her.

A crackle in the brush. The cry of a startled animal. The sound of gunfire. Where on earth was he? Why was he doing this to her? Whatever plans he had for her must be important.

The earth below was prickly upon her skin, and was likely filled with spiders. She wanted desperately to try to free her hands, but was afraid to move in case the man with the gun would hear.

Maybe her parents had offered up her ransom, or the man who was following her was a sheriff and was coming to take her back to her parents! But sheriffs don't shoot down an unarmed man in cold blood. Or do they? Maybe the Mexican had drawn a weapon on him, forcing him to fire.

Desperate for a fix and unable to sleep, her mind filled with questions, Lissy lay shivering in the blackness in fear. It was cold in the thicket, and damp, yet she was perspiring profusely, the dress clinging to her back and armpits.

Picking up his pace while walking towards to the river, the *traficante de rey* whistled softly, guided by the light of the moon and the stars.

When Lissy woke to a noise within the trees, her body on fire, she struggled to her feet without pause, running quickly through the thicket down the river.

– – –

In the high-rise within the heart of the sprawling city, the pieces finally starting to come together, Tha Phah studied the images again and lit up a cigar. The night prior, in full view of those who walked past the parish, angering the mostly-Catholic city, a young girl had been found murdered upon the grounds of the Catholic church of St. Augustine of Angeles, in the Forbes Park region of Makita City. Beneath a breast and encased in spit, wadded up so tight that it was barely visible, had been a card. Even more important, there had been a name and a number scribbled upon it, one which would help bring some justice for the mothers and fathers of murdered sons and daughters, and anyone else who had ever lost a loved one to the violence of the drug wars. The girl had been found in a soiled robe without shoes face-down on the grass, a single gunshot wound to the chest. She had also been covered in sequins and tar.

Due to the obvious foul play and the strange circumstances surrounding her death, the coroner's office had run a battery of tests. It had been thought that she had been just another of Makita's sprawling influx of American and other foreign prostitutes that slinked through the streets selling their sex, killed before they were handed the promised money, but the fact that the girl had been coated in tar and had gone to great lengths to conceal the card, along with the number that had been scribbled upon it, the evidence had mounted for Tha Phah to send his men in. Although the woman had been American, the number upon the card was local and had connected directly to a clinic for needy women, the one in the downtown section of the city that his surveillance equipment was directed upon.

When the tests came back that the girl had been four months pregnant with twins, his suspicions confirmed and a name to go after, that of *Bayanai Rizal*, a self-proclaimed ringleader of the operation, along with smashing a paperweight to bits upon his desk, he was ready to close in. While there were those who didn't care what happened to the young girls and women who became caught up in the sex and drug trades of Makita City and the rest of the Philippines, and those who believed that they deserved it due to their drug addiction and flaunting of their sex, he did care, and better yet, now he finally was in possession of what he needed to show it.

Satisfied with the day's work and with the results of the tests, but distraught over the young girl's death, he studied the scribbled name on the card again.

Bayanai Rizal. Philippine for "hero" of men.

Ah yes. A hero indeed. And one he would meet with an arrest warrant and an iron fist, a Filipino national who was on the nation's most wanted list, a notorious leader of the most wide-spread and exploitive sex ring yet, and someone who he had fervently been trying to hunt-down and convict for over two years. Unable to believe his good fortune, he rubbed his eyes as if the card would disappear.

— — —

Auntie Pam

As the pain increased, Lissy woke to a major headache, something big and wet against her face. Noticing that she had full use of her arms, she struggled to get up, finally free of the tape.

"There, there, chil, done yo move. Yo had yosef a *night!*"

The thick, broken, voice was coming from above, as she strained to see, the cold towel blocking her view. Every bone and muscle ached, and she was burning up. With a groan, she lay back down, trying to remove the towel, but the voice objected, pushing it down on her head again.

"Chil, I wouldn't do dat if I wuz yo. Yo got a nasty bum der, yo do."

Lissy placed a hand to her head, feeling around until she came to the large knot above her right eye. The voice was right. There was a bump there. And it hurt like mad. Trying to focus her eyes in the light, she peered at the hulking shadow that towered over her as if she was a piece of pie. The woman was large, fat, ancient, and black, outfitted in a too-tight dress that didn't fit, and which was fastened at the waist by an apron. She was a character straight out of a childhood storybook, and she talked like one, too. Wondering who the woman was and where she was, Lissy spoke.

"Where am I? And who are you?"

Staring the woman down, Lissy triumphantly threw the towel off.

"Chil, I know dat der is ting's dat is burnin da mind, an I be answering dem juz as soon as ah ken, but yo need yo sleep now, an dat's dat. Yo ken call me Auntie. Auntie Pam. An fo how I found yo, let's juz say dat yo one fortunate chil! Wit dat bum on yo head an yo bein down by da water in dat poison oak, oh, lordie, chil! Auntie Pam got yo out ah der in da *nick* a time! Tank da Lord, I do, chil! Now yo settle yoself back down an Auntie Pam she go fetch yo some toas an jam."

The woman reminded her of the old woman on the front of that pancake box mix, the one dressed in an apron with a kerchief wrapped round her head. She was kind, but strong in voice and tone, and Lissy came to the conclusion that, gentle that she was, that she just didn't understand.

"Thank you, Auntie Pam for your kindness, and I don't want to alarm you, really I don't, but there's someone after me- and he has a gun. And he already shot someone. I have to call my parents and tell them the danger that I'm in, and I have to do it now. They need to be told to come for me, Auntie Pam."

Exasperated, and knowing that at any time that whoever was following her could appear out of nowhere before them, Lissy held back the tears. The woman's hands were upon her hips, and she obviously didn't have a clue what she was trying to tell her at all.

"Chil, like ah said, I know yo don have yo quessions. Auntie Pam she don have no phone, cuz she in da middle of da wooz, and she don have no need fo one. But if yo need ta caw yo mamma…"

As abruptly as she had started, the woman cut herself off and stared up above, crossing herself while singing a song, then patted Lissy's hand.

"My mamma, she wuz one fine woman, she don wuz. Lived here in da wooz til she don gone died on herself. Oh, Lord, now."

Squeezing Lissy's hand a little tighter; she broke into tears, making Lissy, as sore and frightened as she was, and in spite of her situation, very sad.

"Then, Auntie Pam, I'm sure you can understand how important it is that I call my mother now. She has to know that I'm alive. And she has to come get me- now. You have to call for help- you've just got to."

Lissy sat up in the big, fluffy bed and took stock of the fat, red welts that now covered her legs and arms.

Ah, the dreaded poison oak. How she abhorred the stuff! And she had come down with a pretty good case of it as a young girl when she had strayed off a path during a hike that she had taken with a Girl Scout troop.

The woman was as kind as the Mississippi River was long and wide, but she had to make her understand the seriousness of her situation.

"He'll kill you, too, Auntie Pam, if you don't get to a phone right now."

Finally seeming to understand, the woman let Lissy's hand go.

"Chil, yo dem der havin dat evil dreams gan! Yo Auntie Pam, she will caw yo mamma tamarrow when she go ta town. And if yo say, she call da *police* too."

"Please, Auntie Pam, do. Just as soon as you're possibly able. But there has to be a closer phone than town. It's extremely important. That man- he killed someone, and he's after me, and has been ever since the van broke down. I don't know why, or what he wants, but if he knows that you're trying to help me, he'll kill you, too."

She was exasperated, and running out of time. Whoever was following her should have already been there by now, wherever she was. Maybe he was watching them right now. She had to make the woman understand.

"Chil, I de only one here in de wooz now. Der wuz one kine soul by de name ah Puddin, but he don gone meet mamma now, dat's right, he do. Now, I de only one. An tamarrow, I den der go ta town. How da do miss Puddin an dat puddin he der been cookin! Lordy, now!"

Her story told, the woman quieted down, as she resumed rocking back and forth upon the chair that she was sitting upon.

"I'm sorry, Auntie Pam. I didn't mean to pry. But you've got to call for help. He's out there somewhere, and he's coming. Maybe he's already here. He should have been here by now."

Exhausted with trying to argue her case, she lay back down, as Auntie Pam, with a hand to Lissy's forehead to rearrange the towel, left the room to fetch the jam and toast.

The room that Auntie Pam had put her in was cheerful, big and bold, just like Auntie Pam herself. The bed was wide and tall, cherry red and soft, and the curtains that adorned the lone window were yellow and reminded her of the islands, and were tied in neat little bows. The room had so much wood within its walls that she was surprised that Auntie Pam was able to move about it at all. All of the furniture was big and old- antique, no doubt, and trimmed in a shade of avocado. There was no television, just a roll-top desk, the old kind that was used for writing, with a single jade pipe and bag of tobacco on top. And doilies, lace, over all the room. Upon the carpet of gold shag rested a colorful, braided rug, thick as the fat square heels that adorned Auntie Pam's wrinkled ankles. It was indeed a room that Lissy would have felt quite comfortable in, if she hadn't been on the run.

With a heavy sigh, she tried to patiently wait for Auntie Pam's return but nodded off, the nightmare of Trevor returning loud and strong. This time, instead of the burning cornfield, he was standing ablaze upon a churning river, a syringe in hand, as, body melting, he reached out.

"Here, Lis!" he called, as she tore off her clothes from the shore to jump in after him. "I saved some for you!"

Then, with an evil grin, he plunged the syringe deep down into his neck.

"No! Trev! No! Wait! I'm coming to help you!"

Sobbing uncontrollably, she plunged into the churning water as blood poured from his neck and he disappeared beneath the surface. Like every other time that the dream had appeared, and just like in her waking hours, it was too late to try to save him, and he was dead. When Auntie Pam returned to the room, Lissy was moaning and thrashing around.

"Der, der, chil. Yo Auntie Pam's hew."

Soaked in sweat, Lissy woke to another cold towel being placed upon her forehead again.

"Now I don der told yo, chil, yo don go get yo sleep now. Der no one comin fo yo in de wooz now. Yo juz eat yo toas an jam, an yo feel betta, yo do."

Refusing to take 'no' for an answer, Auntie Pam sat and rocked in the old wooden chair while Lissy went about devouring the toast. The round of sourdough was soft and sweet, and the jam was maple and homemade. Feeling a little better but still nauseous, Lissy laid back and listened to the chair creak back and forth across the carpet.

"That was good, Auntie Pam. Can I have some water?"

She was thirsty, and desperate for a fix, because her stomach was cramping up again. Her request for a drink sparked Auntie Pam into song.

"Chil, I dat der go gat yo Auntie Pam's famoose tea, yo hode on, an Auntie Pam der be right back. Yo gone love it, chil."

Returning a few minutes later, a cup of tea in hand, Auntie Pam's eyes glazed over as Lissy drank it up.

The "tea," although it did indeed have tea leaves in it, was comprised of a strange concoction of cottonwood bark and hops that made Lissy, as sick as she was, relax. The more that she sipped the bitter concoction down, the more that she was at peace with the world, and completely at home with Auntie Pam. Everything faded but the large, boisterous woman and the wide, tall room, thoughts of the man with the gun who was after her, and of the Mexican who had fallen dead to the ground now long past. She watched sleepily as Auntie Pam shuffled slowly toward the desk.

Packing the tobacco tight down into the pipe, Auntie Pam lit up, rocking and softly singing a song in a thick, southern accent and broken English that Lissy couldn't understand. Then, her big, fleshy lips around the stem, and with a final puff, as Lissy nodded off, she shuffled slowly back toward the door where she turned off the light, leaving Lissy in darkness.

"Chil, yo don worry yo preddy head, yo hear? Yo Auntie Pam, she be back en da mornin fore she go ta town."

Already sound asleep, Lissy couldn't have cared.

– – –

Lissy woke to a cool breeze blowing through the open window and to Auntie Pam's robust singing as she glided cheerfully into the room, purse in hand. Outfitted in thick stockings and a straw bonnet with plastic birds upon it, her hands were encased in elbow-length gloves. She was on her way to town, and it showed in her walk and her talk.

"Chil, yo draw de water fo yo Auntie Pam now yo hear? Cuz ho hands de be ah dolled up."

Waddling over toward a bucket in the corner, Auntie Pam placed it upon the nightstand near the bed.

"Da fesh air, it be good fo yo, chil. Den yo Auntie Pam, she go."

Gently pushing Lissy in the direction of the back porch and the little garden that held the well, she placed the bucket in her hand, before waddling back over to the desk to remove a glove and to pack the pipe back down.

"Chil, yo Auntie Pam she de neez her smoke. De say da smoke iz de devil, but yo Auntie Pam, she nos betta den dat."

Lissy watched as Auntie Pam sat down to rock again, swaying to and fro, the smoke from the elegant pipe swirling up around her ungloved hand. Content as a cat with a bowl of milk at Sunday service, she groaned loud and long, then broke into song.

At the well, Lissy filled the bucket, drawing up the cool, fresh water from the earth below. It felt good to be outside again, to be among the birds and the honeysuckle that clung to the old well, the grass beneath her feet soft and thick, the garden dotted with wildflowers and silver maples. A butterfly fluttered down upon her hand, wings of prairie yellow resting in the dawn. For a moment, in the silence of the morning, amongst the creatures of the woods and the birds, she felt at home.

As a shot rang out, breaking the silence, Lissy dropped the bucket and bolted through the grass towards the forest and its thick carpet of maple that lay 30 meters from the garden's red brick well. Barefoot and in pajamas, afraid to turn for what she might see, she ran as if there was a gun pointed at her back. Reaching the safety of the trees that blanketed the back woods earth, she zigzagged quickly through the carpet of leaves and white-washed bark, unsure of where to turn, the rough bark and twigs cutting into her feet.

30 meters in the distance and loading his weapon, the *traficante de rey* began closing in on his prey.

Sailing blindly through the trees like a wounded bird, Lissy ran just as fast as she could, unaware of the fallen branch beneath her feet. As she tripped on it, she fell in pain, her leg caught beneath. Struggling to get free, her leg broken or sprained, she heard the brush crackle behind her as she tried to free her leg. Her eyelids were heavy and she was sleepy, more tired than she had ever been, her body in a state of immobility and pain.

It was the end, this forest, this lonely place.

She had been hit, and she was going to die here. At the age of 17. In the forest, in the middle of nowhere, all alone.

The last thing that Lissy saw before she faded away was the *traficante* standing above her, and the rope that he was carrying.

— — —

There are some who say that when the end comes, it will be a fire of brimstone and smoke, but Auntie Pam, and the other down-home folks who resided out in the backwoods along the muddy river that ran from Eastern Mississippi on down to the gulf, believed that when it was time to meet their maker, that it would be upon the wings of a chorus of angels who would carry them victoriously through the pearly gates. True to her churchgoing soul and to all of the peach pies that she used to make for the women's bible study of the Catholic parish that was but a phone call away, when Auntie Pam passed that day, shotgun blast to the back of the head, singing her church songs and smoking her pipe, and when the skies opened up in a display of colors and light, she never knew what hit her, and it was a joyous day indeed.

Makita

The day spent in surveillance of the incoming images from the clinic, Tha Phah studied the evidence. In the last decade especially, clinics like the *Banal na Sanggol* or the 'Holy Infant,' had been growing in number, not just in the Philippines, but in other third-world nations like China and Nigeria. Intent on getting the most 'bang for their money' they operated within a cloak of greed and darkness the cheapest and dirtiest way they were able, targeting young women, especially white ones, to carry and birth babies. Not only did the *pangalawas* or 'surrogates' not have to be paid for their services, saving the going rate of approximately $20,000 per woman, but the girls could be used for toil and multiple purposes, making the operation highly profitable and cost-effective. Add to that the high likelihood of multiple births, sometimes three or more, due to the implantation of multiple embryos and fertility treatments, and for *traficante de reys* like Bayanai Rizal who were in it for financial gain, it was a 'win-win' business. In a nation suffering from governmental and financial oppression, it was much simpler to seek out the desired young women than it was to shell out the $20,000 to the *pangalawas* and *jovencitas* for their services; the procedures provided the selected girls entirely cost effective procedures indeed. The *turistas* and young men who were selected to sire the babies were, like the women, selectively targeted and underpaid, in it for the sex almost as much as the money, walking in, then out, with a little cash in their pockets and a smile, not out anything at all.

For the most part, and unlike in other countries which were more barbaric, and provided that the *chicas* complied, they were not severely mistreated, the opiates and pharmaceuticals provided them freely throughout their 'treatment' causing them to be, for the most part, satisfied and compliant. Escape was something that most of the girls never considered, during the conditioning and 'brainwashing' process; they were told that their families and loved ones would be killed if they even thought about escape. At the *Bahay ng Biyaya*, a *pangalawa* was chained as a last resort, and only if it had been determined that her thoughts were 'evil' and of selfish need. After the initial three week treatment and conditioning process, the girls, freshly drugged and compliant, found themselves almost eager to begin their new life.

The girls at the 'clinics,' and at the *Bahay ng Biyaya,* or 'House of Grace' and other homes like it throughout their stay formed friendships to last a lifetime, provided the opportunity ever arised. They named their offspring, laughed and cried, missed the infants when they were removed from their wombs and taken away, if they were able to remember in the first place. The house masters and *traficantes took* a twisted pride in the young women under their wing, often taking on the role of an 'uncle' or grandfather figure to their girls during their stay- the most fertile *pangalawas* provided with small tokens of appreciation like chewing gum and candy. After years of toil and baby-making, and when it was time for a *jovencita* to leave her *'familia'* permanently, the women cried and composed cards of friendship and love, etched in coal upon bamboo, in remembrance of friendships made. A *pangalawa* entered the brothels and clinics a girl, and exited a woman of experience and age.

For the most part, the 'clinics' and houses ran effectively, coming under surveillance or into the news only if a young woman was discovered dead somewhere, in which case, after months or even years of investigation and surveillance, there would be a raid. Sadly, more times often than not, and to the great frustration of good men like Tha Phah, the clinics quickly opened up again in another region of the city under different 'ownership' and name. It was a lucrative business, one difficult to eradicate and restrain, and one which paid highly. The operations literally bled out money, monies critical for the purchasing power and ongoing operations of the drug trade. As babies were birthed and sold, drug trades were made, hundreds upon thousands of dollars crossing hands and national lines in the name of methamphetamine, heroin, hashish, and crack cocaine.

In the business of flushing out illegal sex trade and baby-making operations for nearly a decade, Tha Phah despised the despicable trade, partly for the fact that he was a father himself to two little girls, with another child on the way. Knowing that there were men out there who were targeting young women, children really, for their birthing capabilities and for money for the drug trade made him sick to his stomach. The more *traficante de reys* and pushers that he took off the streets, the better that he could sleep at night, literally. And if he could put men like Bayanai Rizal behind bars, well, better yet. The *turistas* and other young men like them who hopped flights from Australia and the Americas to the Philippines he wasn't personally interested in prosecuting, at least on the federal level, as he had bigger busts to make. In all actuality, they were but boys, in it for the sex as much as the money, enticed into the business with the flash of a bill, before they knew what was even happening. No, the *turistas* he would leave to the local police, gathering up names which he handed over gladly.

Tha Phah studied the images impatiently, a phone call away from initiating the raid, trying to get a feel for the activities and appearances of Rizal, if he ever came. He would come down on the clinic only when the *traficante de rey* made his entrance, and not until. He had waited this long, and he would wait a lifetime, if need be, just for the satisfaction of nailing him. Until now, he had seen the Filipino kingpin enter the clinic only once, and at that time his role in the trade had yet to be determined, and he had not been ready anyway. Now, it had been almost 12 weeks since the *traficante* had come around, and Tha Phah, for all his patience, was growing quickly impatient. He wanted to see the trafficker behind bars for life, or better yet, done away with by one of the other prisoners while behind them, because of the crimes he had committed against humanity. Yet, unfortunately for the sex and other illegal trades under the government of the Philippines, 16 years was the maximum punishment for involvement, something that he desperately wanted to change. Even a lifetime sentence couldn't make up for what the *jovencitas* were put through for money. The years of toil and abuse took their tremendous toll on the women, and Tha Phah had made it his life's work to try to alleviate their suffering. He would make sure that the phony 'clinic' was shut down, and he would go after it and others like it again, and again, and again, until the government cracked down on the baby-making operation itself and initiated stricter penalties. Anxious for Rizal to show, Tha Phah lit a cigar, and then another, before calling his wife as the sun set upon the city.

In a wheelchair beside her captor in a first class seat, Lissy, bound at the legs beneath a long dress so that no one would see, drugged with opiates to assure compliancy and inability to speak, sat like the good young bride that she was on the 18 hour flight from Mississippi to Makita City, her mental illness documented and verified. The *traficante* beside her was sullen and displeased- not only had he had to arrange another flight, but Rizal had come down on him, punishing him with a forthcoming 50% reduction of his monies, for the time that it had taken him to capture Lissy in the woods behind the well. With a kiss to his new bride's cheek, he squeezed her hand in an obligatory fashion, and then ordered another drink. Lissy endured the long flight the best that she was able, confined to the wheelchair and unable to speak. When the aircraft arrived in Makita City, it was almost a good thing, as the *traficante* wheeled her off the plane and into the waiting jeep.

– – –

While on the flight from Mississippi to Makita City, Lissy had been able to see, on the ride from the airport to the clinic, a cloth was tied around her face. The *traficante* spoke urgently, briefly, in a dialect that she couldn't understand, the jeep speeding quickly down the highway. Upon arrival, the blindfold was removed and she was strapped to the wheelchair and wheeled up the concrete, the drugs still rendering her unable to speak. Terrified, she struggled to identify her surroundings for anything which might give her place of imprisonment away, seeing only the ancient stone structure before her, and the street. The building was in a state of disrepair, looming and grey, the nameplate upon the door faded and unreadable.

As she was wheeled toward the clinic, the heat of the city greeted her face, warm and dry as was customary for an early September day, the vehicles passing by a surreal parade. She fought to scream so that someone might hear, but nothing came out of her throat, only air. No sooner was she inside that the wheelchair stopped abruptly, a man of Philippine nationality studying her face. Stooping down, he pinched a cheek, and then the other, and then a leg, sliding a finger down the length of her nose while running a hand through Lissy's silky mane.

Ito ay isang mahusay na isa, ditto. Kumuha ng kanyang handa. "We have a good one here. Get her ready."

Obeying orders, the *traficante* wheeled her quickly toward the exam table as Lissy stared in fright at the paper gowns and surgical equipment. After another round of orders which she couldn't understand, she was hoisted upon the table in preparation for her blood work and exam. Terrified and unable to speak, she fought to remain conscious while 7 vials of blood was taken and her temperature recorded, a blood pressure cuff strapped securely to her upper arm. Inflated much too tightly, the cuff cut off the circulation until it was taken away. She watched in horror as the clinic 'physician' slipped on gloves and readied the syringe of medication that would begin the detox process. At the *Banal na Sanggol*, there was no time wasted for anything. Every day, every hour, every minute, every second of every ovarian cycle, there was money to be made. Not bothering to look at Lissy, the 'physician' injected her with the pharmaceuticals that would begin her withdrawal.

Ito ay isang malusog na batang bagay. Niya gawin lamang fine. Lumabas ang kanyang malayo. "This one is a healthy young thing. She'll do just fine. Take her away."

Un-gagged, but still bound at the knees, Lissy was placed back in the wheelchair for the hour-long journey to the *Bahay ng Biyaya* or 'House of Grace,' where the injections would be continued three to four times around the clock throughout the day until the meth that she had ingested was out of her system entirely. Three weeks later to the day, she would be taken back to the clinic to be injected with the progesterone and other pharmaceuticals that would ready her uterus for acceptance of the egg. No later than 12 days later, and if the implantation was successful, she would be allowed to 'wait out' the remainder of her nine month pregnancy, servicing the *turistas* as they came, and if it wasn't, fertility treatments would be initiated back at the clinic with the goal of a multiple birth. If fertilization still didn't occur after a period of 12 months, the *pangalawa* began the humiliating but financially necessary process of servicing an even greater number of *turistas* so as to initiate pregnancy. As with the other *pangalawas,* the *jovencitas* would be serviced out right up until the last two weeks of their pregnancy. Rizal ran a tight machine, one around which fortunes were made, and one which the *Banal na Sanggol* was determined to keep- no room for resistance, mistakes, or sleep.

As she was re-blindfolded for the ride back to the brothel, the tears came, and with no clue where she was or what she had been given, Lissy's heart beat like a wounded train on the hour's ride from the *Banal na Sanggol Medikal to* the *Bahay ng Biyaya*, where the jeep stopped and deposited its newest *pangalawa* with a calculated ease. Terrified at the thought of what they would do to her, Lissy struggled to remain conscious as she was ushered inside a small room reserved for the *pangalawas* who were either ill, or menstruating. Unbeknown to her, the fact that she was in cycle would keep her untouched and safe, at least for a few days.

Pangalawa

Left alone for the first time in days, Lissy surveyed her surroundings. There were no windows in the small room, or furniture. Inside the barren walls upon the floor were seven other girls, engaged in either quiet discussion, game-playing, or disengagement. Considering their circumstances, they seemed fairly content, and didn't appear to be underfed or mistreated. The youngest one, a girl of about 14, expressed interest in Lissy, the newest *pangalawa* of the *Bahay ng Biyaya* with a shy smile. From what Lissy could tell, the girls ranged in age from approximately 14 to 17, with Lissy possibly the oldest. Like Lissy, they were outfitted in identical thin cloth robes, and were barefoot. The girl who had greeted her was holding something in her hand, which she now offered to Lissy in an open palm, revealing a rubber ball and jack which, until now, Lissy had never played with. Forgetting herself for a moment, Lissy bounced the ball and then caught it, then placed it back into the young girl's hand. What she noticed was that there appeared to be a certain comradery between the girls, even given their situation.

The simple game and others like it continued, as she engaged in childish play that until now she had seen only in old magazines- jacks, dice, games with string, and other hand games, relieving some of her anxiety and boredom. The girls seemed oblivious to anything other than the game they were playing, until a silent figure of foreign descent appeared briefly to switch off the overhead bulb, leaving them in darkness. As if on que, all talking stopped, and there was silence. The room now dark and cold, the girls began drifting off to various sections of the wall, motioning for Lissy to do the same. She spent the long night wide awake in the dark space huddled against a cold wall; the only heat the bodies of the nearby girls, as she listened to their cries and then, to their snoring.

Thirty minutes before dawn, sore from a night spent on the stone floor, she was ushered along with the seven girls into another room, one with a long table and benches, to join more girls, all in varying stages of pregnancy, where she was fed a small meal consisting of water, some type of foul-smelling paste that she couldn't decipher, and crackers. The paste was dry and tasteless, but she spread it upon the crackers, famished. In a corner a man stood guard, as the girls ate in silence.

Expected to follow suit without disobedience or question, after the meal she followed along behind the girls who had been in her room, in preparation for daily toil in the fields. There she was provided with a hoe and basket, as she followed the girls into the long, narrow rows of vegetables. She spent the day pulling weeds from a cabbage field, placing the largest heads into the basket. At day's end and upon dark, they were ushered inside where they unloaded the baskets, after which they were herded off to the gathering room again, and served an evening meal of water, paste, rice, and oatmeal. Although her stomach was cramping and she was in need of a fix, and although the new medications had been started to begin the detox process, she ate without protest, after which she and the seven other *pangalawas* who were in cycle were ushered back into the windowless room again. An hour later she lay pressed against the wall and cement, fearful and exhausted.

The same routine went on for four days, during which some of the girls were removed, and new ones were brought in. Twice a day, in the field, and during breaks for water, the girls were examined to see if they were still in cycle, after which they were either transported to the clinic or returned to the field. While picking the vegetables, the girls remained mandatorily quiet, due to the presence of an armed guard several rows behind them. If one of the girls tried to rest, even for a second, a gruff, foreign voice would urge her to keep going.

It was before lights out and after the nightly meal that Lissy got to know the girls, and of their courage and bravery. During her time there, she listened to stories of what went on in the other rooms, and why, and how, during the night, that the walls would come alive in motion. The thought of being used as a *pangalawa* or surrogate seemed surreal and terrified Lissy, and worse was the thought of being turned out for 'service.' She found it hard to believe what the girls were telling her; it seemed incredulous that there were really people out there who would take advantage of people like the *traficantes* at the *Bahay ng Biyaya* were claimed to do. Restless and unable to sleep, her mind filled with questions.

Where was she? How long would she be here? Why was she selected over others? How could she tell her parents that she was alive?

On the fifth day, and after her cycle had ended, she was 'turned out' into yet another room specifically for the *jovencitas* who were in detox. Here she would spend the remaining 16 days of her three week initiation as the meth fully left her body, after which she would be taken back to the clinic to be implanted with a single human embryo. Assuming that the results were positive, she would be taken to the early stage pregnancy room, where, along with daily toil in the fields, her stomach would ripen like a melon, provided that the implantation proved successful. On consecutive implantations, and provided that the birth had been without major complications or problems, two embryos would be implanted for the rest of her duration at the brothel- one male, and one female. And if she was able to tolerate the multiple pregnancies and births well, she would be regarded as being highly fertile, after which she would be implanted annually from there on out with a minimum of three or more embryos.

From her third year on, as told by the girls, the next 7 years within the *Bahay ng Biyaya* or House of Grace would roll slowly and methodically by as she birthed *bambinos* for sale, until, now a young woman of 27, she would be sold into foreign labor and 'employment.' It was a selective business, one which Rizal and the men like him who ran it went to great lengths to elicit monies for the drug trade for the truckloads and tons of illegal drugs that were shipped out by freighter to Europe and the Americas.

In the second room, the girls were ill, in varying stages of detox. Unlike the first room that Lissy had spent time in, there was always a man on guard in a corner. Here, the girls cried and vomited, shivered and shook, hit their heads against the walls, lashed out at anyone and everything, swore and screamed out, until the pharmaceuticals took over and 'righted their minds,' calming them and making them feel good again, whatever drug or drugs that they had previously ingested now finally out of their systems. Most of the girls were too ill to move, and didn't talk. The ones who did relayed to Lissy stories of unbelievable horror and suffering- girls who had died while in detox and from the heavy medication given them, during childbirth and labor, and of the *pangalawas* who never returned from the clinic at all.

Forced to hoe the cabbage fields during her waking hours, at lights out sleep was impossible, the sounds that the exhausted girls emitted piteous and animal. Lissy spent the next 16 days pulling weeds and vomiting the contents of her stomach up- chunks of paste and rotten vegetables, crackers, unable to keep anything down. At night while lying on the stones she listened to the sounds that came from the walls, and of the grunts of male voices. Afraid to talk or move, least she called attention to herself; she remained sick and dumb, like the rest of the girls. On the dawn of the 16th day, and just when she was beginning to feel a little better, she was fed a meal of canned meat and crackers, placed back into the jeep, and transferred. On the ride over, and after being shot up with a hallucinogenic, Lissy fell asleep for the first real time in 9 days, visions of girls with swollen melon bellies in varying stages of pregnancy and labor writhing and moaning in her head.

Back at the clinic, she was wheeled back into the perfunctory room and given the series of injections, one of them the endometrial thickening progesterone. During the entire time the 'physician' was silent, looking at Lissy only to nod his head, poke or prod, or to motion for her to sit up or lay down. From what she had learned from the girls, the injections given were to prepare her uterus for the implantation, thickening the endometrial and vaginal walls, after which she would be implanted with the single embryo. Then, back to the *Bahay ng Biyaya* or House of Grace she would go, where, 9 days later, and up until 12 days after implantation, she would be tested for the desired pregnancy.

The injections finished, and the exam completed, stunned and exhausted, she was bound again at the feet and wheeled back out for the ride 'home.' That evening, back in the room, she sat sobbing in a corner.

"It isn't so bad. You'll get through it. We all do."

Lissy looked up to see who was talking to her, the soft voice coming from one of the older girls.

"No one stays here forever," the girl said, attempting to make her feel better. "One day they let you out."

Lissy stared through her tears at the gentle creature before her, a pretty girl with ivory skin and hair the color of coral. Not believing a word of what she said, she spoke.

"I'll believe it when I see it," Lissy said. "I don't want to be here at all. I want to go home."

"There isn't any going home," the girl told her. "At least, I don't think so. Did they take you out behind the fields? " she asked Lissy with wide eyes. "Did they show you what happens to the girls that try to leave here?"

Yes, how could she forget what lay out behind the rows of cabbage and potatoes. Not even a stick marked the graves of the girls who lay there.

"Yes, I saw the field," Lissy answered. "Don't worry, I'm not going anywhere, they told me that they would kill my parents if they even thought that I wanted out of here."

"Just wait," the girl said. "Wait out your time here. Once they sell you out, it won't be bad at all."

It wouldn't be bad? Right! She didn't believe it for a second.

The girl looked at her blankly, her face sagging and sallow. Unable to guess her age, Lissy propped herself up against the wall and stared at the girl.

"I don't want to be sold; I just want to go home. My parents probably think that I'm dead, and I miss them."

She sneezed, shaking her head at the girl. The room was drafty, just like the other, and no doubt the next surprise would be that she would come down with a cold or pneumonia.

"Well, if you need someone to talk to, I'm here," the girl told her. "But really, it isn't that bad, this is my tenth pregnancy, and after it's over, I'll have birthed 19 babies for the *traficantes*. I haven't been allowed to see any of them, at least, not just yet, but each time they tell me what I had before they send me back here. I give them names, remember their birthdays, everything. Just like a real mother would do. The last time I was at the clinic I was told that I'll be sold out in just two more years. Four more births- and I can do it. It isn't that bad, the only part that really hurts is the labor. But sometimes they induce you, which helps, because it makes the baby come quicker. And if you're really lucky, they'll take it by caesarian. Besides, the *turistas* in that back room," she whispered as she pointed behind her. "Once they know that you're pregnant, if you treat them well, they'll bring you things, all the time. Things that will make the time here go by a lot quicker. Like magazines and candy."

Lissy's heart broke for the girl. She had never felt sadder in all her life. The *pangalawa* with the coral halo of hair and jade eyes was with child, about three or four months along.

"One of my pregnancies was by a *turista*," the girl said, her eyes glassy. "All of the other times I've been able to become pregnant by fertilization and implantation. And do you know what? Although I was worried about being serviced out at first, it wasn't bad at all. I was able to become pregnant after only three months back there. I know which one of them did it," she whispered, glancing around as if the *traficante* who was on guard might hear and come around. "He was a tall, dark, Australian boy of 23, and his name was 'James.' He said he wanted to marry me, and I believe him. He said he'll be waiting for me when I get out of here, and that he's going to offer to buy me, if he can come up with the money. Do you think he'll be able to come up with it?" she asked. "He has two more years."

"He'll come up with it," Lissy said softly, feeling sorrier for the poor girl by the minute. "And I'm glad for you. How old are you?" she asked. "And what's your name? My name is Elizabeth, but everyone calls me Lissy, and I'm 17."

"24," the girl answered, rubbing her stomach tenderly. "My name is Harmony."

24? And already have given birth to 17 babies? How was that even possible? The poor, poor child.

Lissy, although she was seven years younger, suddenly felt like an adult talking to a desperate child.

Maybe that's what the drugs they gave were for. To mess with your head.

She felt incredibly sorry for the girl, getting up to put an arm around her.

"How old were you when they brought you here, Harmony?"

Such a young life full of only suffering and pain. She couldn't believe it. She didn't believe it. This was all just a bad dream, and any second, she would wake up.

"I was 12. One of the younger ones," she said with a soft laugh. You're lucky, Lissy."

Suddenly ill, Lissy threw up. She wanted out, and she wanted out now. Her parents had to be worried sick about her.

"Yes," she repeated. "I guess that I am."

"Look" she told Harmony. "I'm not going to let them do this to me. I'll refuse to eat. And if I'm pregnant from their implantation, I'll starve myself. You can't have a baby if you starve yourself."

That's exactly what she would do. She would feign sickness, mental illness, something.

"Trust me, they're wise to that, and it won't work," Harmony answered. "There are girls who have tried it, and the *traficantes* are right on it. If you try to starve yourself, they'll force feed you. Through a tube, and they'll tie you down for your entire pregnancy, too. You'll wish you were dead out behind the field. I've seen it. I've seen what they do to those girls. I've heard their screams, too."

"Then I'll just kill myself," said Lissy. "I can't be here."

"None of us want to be here," said Harmony. "You don't understand. You can't do yourself in, you can't do anything. The only thing you can do is keep your mouth shut and grow their embryos. And count the days until they let you out. If you're really serious about dying, then run away. You've seen what happens to the girls who try it."

"Well," said Lissy. "I don't believe it. I don't think there's really anybody buried out there, and I think that they just take us out there behind the field to scare us."

"Believe it," said Harmony. "It's true. Just do what they tell you. Make friends with your *turistas*. Give them what they want, and take their affections and candy. And work hard in the fields. Before you know it, you'll be on your way to somewhere else. Look at me, my time here is almost done," she said, hands upon her stomach. "And the best part is that during the last two weeks of this pregnancy, is that I'll have a chance to induce labor by servicing the *turistas*, and then they won't have to give me their drugs. I've heard that the medicine they give you to induce labor makes you really sick, Lissy. Oh! And I almost forgot! The last four weeks they feed you dried meat to fatten the baby up."

"That sounds horrible," said Lissy, still refusing to believe. "How do you even know it's true what they're telling you? That we'll be sold out? They probably just dump us in the field."

"No," said Harmony. "We're sold out. They get money for all of this, remember? Big money! Not as big as for birthing their babies, but big enough. We're valuable to them, which is why they take care of us. We serve multiple purposes, and we do it well. We're almost irreplaceable, Lissy."

"Yes, I can see," said Lissy. "Such good care indeed. Fish paste and crackers. Well, this is one implantation that isn't going to be successful. I don't want to have a baby now. I'm only 17. And I'll do everything in my power to keep them from doing this to me."

Where was she? Maybe Harmony knew. It was the first step to getting out.

"It's not in your best interests to think like you do," said Harmony. "If they get wind that you're not agreeable, forget about ever going outside again, and forget about just poking at the ground with a hoe. They'll put you in that back room, and then, when you're good and worn out, they'll haul you off to the brothels. And you won't be given any 'feel good' drugs. I've heard that in the servicing rooms in the brothels that the *turistas* just keep on coming and *never* leave you alone. It's completely different than just carrying an embryo or two. The girls who are sent there don't come out for months. Months," she said, as she rubbed her swollen middle. "And if that doesn't work to impregnate you and settle you down, they ship you off into the city, where, trust me, they barely feed you and you'll never get out."

"I'm going to get out somehow," said Lissy. "I won't grow their embryos, and I won't be serviced out or sent away to the brothels. I'll take my chances at getting out."

"There is no escape," whispered Harmony. "The girls who are sent to the city brothels are abused and barely fed a meal. They don't care what happens to you when you're in the brothels. Look at it this way, like I do. All we have to do is to become pregnant and carry their embryos. Simple. Pretty soon, it will be like breathing to you. The brothel girls live in filth and scum and are beaten and abused until they're killed, or until they wear out. There are no tourists or treats, or scraps of meat upon birth and fertilization. Please, Lissy, if you know what's good for you, you'll bide your time here, like I do."

Squeezing Lissy's hand, she settled into a corner upon the cold stones to sleep, hands upon her melon middle.

"Besides," she whispered as she started to doze. "You'll make friends here. The drugs they give you will bring you higher than you've ever flown before. It's a glorious thing, Lissy. Give it another week, you'll see. You'll have a new way of thinking. You won't even know or care that you're pregnant. Your life will be one glorious high to the next, and it's all that you'll care about. They're something else," she mumbled as she drifted off. "Some powerful and mind-blowing stuff. I don't know what they give us, but it's the best stuff in the world. Four times a day," she murmured. "Like clockwork, if you can handle it, for as long as you obey. Just think, Lissy. Nowhere to go, nothing to do, but to get the best high of your life on those bastards for free. So what if they make you pop out a baby every now and then? Every nine months isn't much at all. There's worse things in the world, trust me."

With one last rub to her melon belly, and before Lissy could ask where she was, Harmony fell asleep.

Lissy's dreams that night were fearful and drug-induced, the pharmaceuticals that the *traficantes* had given her kicking in, as she tossed and turned upon the stones. It was summer in Lake Tahoe two years ago and Trevor was there, and she was pregnant with his child. But he was angry, and didn't want her to keep it, making her abort it with a length of wire. Bruised and bleeding, she had swum out into the water just as far as she could go, Trevor calling after, letting the icy cold soothe her injured womb and soul. She swam until she could swim no longer and the lake swallowed her up as she disappeared into the depths below. The last thing that she saw before she drowned was a lavender swan upon a ring of fire at the surface of the water, as she sunk down. As she sunk, the lake froze, and then cracked, the ice trapping her within its cocoon. She woke in a cold sweat, with one of the *traficantes* standing above her, syringe in hand, as he methodically guided the needle into her arm. As she drifted off, she thought about how much she loved white cheese, and how if it was aged too long that it lost all of its flavor and smell, and then it wasn't good anymore. Even cheese from Irish cows, cheese for girls with swollen bellies and coral hair.

Within minutes, Lissy was in dreamland again, and this time, she wasn't cold. When she woke, instead of worrying about the implantation and if she would become pregnant, she was already craving her next injection. The next night, four injections later and the medication finally taking effect, her dreams were peaceful, her upcoming implantation and duties as a *pangalawa* not much of an issue at all, the pharmaceuticals being given her some pretty powerful stuff.

--- --- ---

My dearest Lissy,

I hope that the moon dust is bringing you sweet dreams. I know that if it works for your grandmother Lil, that it will work for you, too. Just make sure that you tie the bag tight each night so that the moon dust doesn't escape and then it will always be there for you, forever and ever. I wasn't going to say this, but you'll have to forgive me for starting to panic. It's been 21 days since I've heard from you. That's a full three weeks, Lissy.

Is 21 the magic number or something? Is 3 weeks when it all falls apart? Then God help me. Are you hurt? Are you ill? Are you on your way home?

Your father keeps assuring me that you'll be home soon, just as soon as you are ready. He says that there's some things that you have to work out that require you to be away from us right now. I believe him, and I believe that you're safe; it's just hard to have you not here with us. School starts up again soon, and I know how excited you are for your junior year.

Just one more year and you'll be out of high school! Imagine that! I still think of you as my little girl, the girl that wears those curly, little hot-glued bows that I used to make for you so many years ago. Do you remember, Lissy? Those days bring such smiles to my face, and I hope to yours, too. Childhood is but a word upon the page until that page moves.

I know that it's hard for you to understand the way that I worry about you, but it's something that just happens, like the turning of a page. There's this blank page and clean slate without any ink, then with each small fleck of ink the page grows and grows until it can hold no more, so great that it has to give way. And when it gives way for the last time, then and only then you'll understand what I'm talking about and the power of the world will be for you, and you'll dip your pen into your own inkwell, just like my mother, your grandmother Lil, and her mother, your great-grandmother Clovis did so many years ago in Mallow. And along the way while you dot your i's and dip your pen into the inkwell, sometimes there won't be any ink, and sometimes there will.

When there's no ink to be found, or the ink dries too quickly upon the page, that's when you might have a little trouble sleeping, like me, and maybe you'll worry too much, too, and that's when you'll get the moon dust out from its hiding place and charge your batteries again. When there's lots of ink, and you roam quickly and free, many things will happen and times will be good for you, as you dot your i's and cross your T's in a pace that quickly fills the page. And that's when you'll know that it's time to stop and slow down just a little, to savor the breath of the day.

And Lissy, along your way you'll laugh, you'll cry, you'll search for falling stars and catch rain with

246

your tongue from the sky, and then one day you'll find yourself sprinkling just a little more moon dust on your pillow because you need just a little more sleep. And then you'll walk down to the creek at night when the moon dances on the water and is full in the sky, because that's when conditions to catch a little moon dust are right. And maybe, just maybe, you'll be lucky enough to cross paths with a deer that talks, which is a rare sight.

And that's when next time that you visit the creek, that you'll tell your little girl, and you'll know what your grandmother and your great-grandmother knew, and her mother, too, that no matter where you are or what you do that you will always be loved and that there will always be a little moon dust to guide your dreams and to brighten up your sky.

I don't know if that helps you to understand, but I hope so.

I love you, Lissy, and I pray that you're alright.

Come home soon,

I love you and I miss you so much,

Mom.

Salakayin

Finally feeling good again, the effects of the hallucinogenics settling in, the remaining days of her detox passed without incident and quickly. The routine of hoeing vegetables in the fields, the thrice- daily progesterone injections to thicken her uterus, and injections of the pharmaceuticals that assured her compliancy left her feeling tired and comfortable. A strategic and heavy form of mind-control, Lissy found herself, after she was feeling better and no longer vomiting her stomach contents up, craving her next injections like crazy, any disobedient thoughts completely out of her system. On the dawn of the 21st day, right on schedule, and right after her morning meal, she was readied for transport back to the *Banal na Sanggol Medikal Klinika*, for the surgical procedure to receive the single embryo to her uterine wall.

Her first surrogacy upon her, dazed and giddy from another injection of drugs, she was bound and wheeled into the waiting vehicle, yet unlike the previous ride in which she was terrified and confused, and desperate to get out, she floated along in the jeep with a sleepy, glazed smile. As the jeep drove along, she found herself almost looking forward to what would happen within the familiar confines of the stark exam room. As one of the *pangalawas* had told her during detox while she was coming down, she had been selected to give the world a very special gift, that of life and the miracle of birth. It wasn't the life that she had planned and dreamed of as a child, but there was nothing she could do about it now. Besides, if she looked at it the way that Harmony did, carrying a child and giving it the gift of life was a beautiful thing. She could do this. She would do this. She had to. There was no other choice available.

Dizzy, but feeling alright, she was wheeled out.

In an older vehicle, one which blended well with the demographic makeup and economics of the city, approximately 40 meters back from the *Banal na Sanggol*; Tha Phah did what he normally did every day that he wasn't pouring over papers at the high rise in the city, which was watching the clinic for any sign of Rizal. The last illegal operation and sex ring that he had busted had been in Manila about six months ago, and he was eager to bust another up. Operating as a massage parlor, it had taken him only two weeks to shut it down.   There had been no involvement with drugs or child prostitution, at least not from what the evidence had turned out, but the illegal business of sex for sale, even for the sexually-forward nation, was still a big 'no-no.' Tracking the Filipino men and the tourists who had entered the building, he had brought his men down upon it the first chance he was able, after one of his officers had successfully passed himself off as one of the parlor's new clientele.

His loathing and hatred for the illegal sex trades was causing him to despise the Philippines itself and was increasing by the day, the local government unwilling or unable to get involved, and with a vast majority of the law corrupt itself. He was quickly tiring of all the filth and scum, and it was becoming just too hard to fight the higher-ups. The men that he imprisoned were quickly let out, back on the streets to sell more sex and drugs. Recently, he had heard on a broadcast of the national news how there were anywhere from 2 million to 12 million youths annually who were either addicted to drugs, exploited, or sexually targeted, a number he found sickening, and hard to fathom at all. He wanted this low-life Bayanai Rizal, and he wanted him bad. Hero- bah! The Filipino kingpin was nothing but rotting, stinking scum. Gutter water. Filth. Plain and simple.

Today, like every morning, his eyes were fastened upon the cameras and upon the clinic itself, as he drank cold instant coffee and lit another smoke. So far, Rizal was a no-show. In the last week, two girls had been wheeled in, and two had been wheeled out. He found the entire operation exceedingly strange, and could hardly wait to bust it up. This operation was different- somehow. Coughing on the cigar, and upon arrival of a jeep in front of the clinic, his eyes lit up. Maybe, he would finally have his man, and he could call out for backup. He watched in anticipation as a young girl was wheeled out, then up the steps, her face glazed and dull. So far, no Rizal. But there was something familiar about the girl, something he couldn't quite put his finger on, either that, or the job was finally wearing him down. No doubt it's just that she was identical to all of the others who had come and gone, which therein would lay the familiarity itself.

Damn, he was tired. And he needed to go home. Do normal stuff. Sit down to dinner with his lovely daughters and loving wife, maybe watch a few reruns of "Hawaii Five O," or "Cops," before going to bed- the usual stuff.

Chugging the coffee down, and running the tape back, he tried to think what was bothering him, what was wrong.

This girl was just like all the others, dressed in the full-length robe, legs planted firmly down, glazed, dopy expression, hair held back with a headband...

A headband? The headband! That was it! None of the other girls on his watch had been wearing anything in their hair!

And then it came to him, where he had seen the girl before, or at least the headband. After 7 long frustrating months of surveillance, he finally had them; the dirty bastards had slipped up. This was one young girl who wasn't being wheeled in for an 'examination,' or at least not the kind of examination that the clinic was licensed to perform.

Knocking over the coffee, his fingers flew over the keyboard as he brought the web page up. It was his lucky day, and he wouldn't be waiting for Rizal to bring the clinic down. Another little something that he did every day, right after he stirred his coffee and called his lovely wife, was to consult the new images which had gone up of missing and exploited children on the website of The National Center for Missing and Exploited Children. The site was created so that anyone, anywhere, could search by name, age, country, state, sex, and race, and now, lo and behold, before his very eyes staring straight at him on the home page was a girl- with the telltale headband, long, silky hair and straight, white teeth, and a beautiful smile. Heart racing, he read the name and caption below the image.

Elizabeth Desiree Harding Boman, age 17, reported as missing from El Paso, Texas, August 15. Mother's name Marie, father's name Steven, no siblings. Suspected runaway.

Runaway his ass!

His mind on overdrive, he placed a call to his superior, and then one to the center's Texas headquarters. Next, he phoned the girl's parents, relaying the message that their only child was alive, leaving out any specifics which might cause them more alarm. Upon hearing the news that Lissy had been found, Marie broke into tears and fell unconscious into Steven's waiting arms.

Tha Phah was flying now- higher than he had flown for awhile. This was turning out to be a major bust. The girl, Elizabeth, or Lissy, as she was affectionately called, had been wheeled in a full 5 minutes ago, and he would have to act fast, and act now. Or wait. Until the next time that she was brought to the clinic, which might or might not happen.

But would there be a next time? What if things didn't go as scheduled, or planned? Would he ever be able to forgive himself if something went wrong? The parents were counting on him to bring their little girl home.

Drenched in perspiration, head in his hands, Tha Phah sought desperately to devise a plan. He could rush the clinic right now, at this very minute, with no back up, and take a chance with who or what was inside, or he could call for backup and then go in. Or, he could wait. And then again, he could follow the jeep after it had reloaded its cargo. Agonizing over what to do, Tha Phah made the decision to call for backup, after which he would follow behind the jeep, with the girl in it, to wherever it was headed to. Now, it was all coming together, and making sense, after the long months of one too many missed meals and time spent away from home. With any luck, the jeep would lead him directly to Rizal, and he could slam his filthy ass directly into a jail cell. He hated these creeps. He hated them all. Sure, if he followed the jeep, there was always the chance that he'd be seen, but it was the option that could lead him to Rizal. If he blew down the clinic doors now with the bastards inside, whoever was there would call Rizal and his stooges, and quite possibly even gun down the girl. No witnesses, no survivors. No, it wasn't the right move if he was going to go in for the kill. He had to take them out in the open, off their guard, not within the clinic walls.

Lighting up a cigar, he got busy making calls as the clinic's 'physician' and resident *traficante* readied Lissy to receive the embryo. To make the procedure just a little easier on her, and to assure her compliancy, he drew up an extra cc of medication into the syringe as he swabbed down her arm. The *traficante* and Rizal's right hand man immensely enjoyed this part of his job, implanting the 'lucky' *pangalawas* as they were wheeled in, and playing God. It was his second favorite part. His first and very favorite was injecting the Pitocin to induce the labor that would deliver the *bambinos*. He considered himself fortunate in all aspects of his employment, and it showed in his pride for his *bebe fabricantes* or baby makers.

After making sure that Lissy's legs were secured to the straps and that she was sufficiently out, he walked proudly into the other room and over to a drawer to retrieve a can of chopped meat that he would reward her with for being with child.

His *pangalawas* were all such good *jovencitas,* and they made him very proud. One day, they just might return to thank him.

— — —

Feliz cumpleanos a ti! Feliz cumpleanos a ti! Feliz cumpleanos quenda hija! Feliz cumpleanos a ti!

There are those who say that in Juarez, there are no innocent victims, and that each loss of life is due to some involvement, no matter how small, in the drug wars. These are the same individuals who attest that the mass grave site where Caesar Sanchez boiled and buried his thousands of victims has no identifiable remains at all. Christened the *sopa de fabricante* or the 'soup maker' he is alive and well, attending the same functions and sitting at the same tables of Mexican government officials, and is still at large.

180 miles west of Chihuahua, down a dirt road branching off from Federal Highway 16, deep within the pines and rocks, far from the bloody violence of Ciudad, Juarez, around the benches placed round, a small gathering sang a happy little song, for the joy and hope that is life, and for all that was right with the world in a world of so much suffering and wrong. One of the highest points on earth and surrounded by cascading waterfalls, the small community of Basaseachi Falls was home to one of Mexico's many Catholic orphanages. Now, as the celebration got underway and the cake was cut, the onlookers clapping long and loud, the Head Mother of *Los Ninos Perdidos* orphanage or "The Lost Children," praised the Lord as she blessed the excited child. It was a double celebration and a happy day indeed.

Feliz cumpleanos! "Happy Birthday!" *Te extranaremos mucho mi nijo!* "We will miss you dearly, my child," the Head Mother said.

The child was being adopted out, one of the lucky at the orphanage in a country who could not afford to care for her own, into a loving home. Not an infant or even a toddler any longer, the angelic girl with the chubby cheeks and raven locks giggled as the Head Mother tossed her the ball. She had come to the orphanage on the wings of the angels, was the tale told by the nun to all, and she was leaving on them as well. In actuality, one of the Mexican *federales* who patrolled the Juarez/United States border had scooped her up in a vacant field, hysterical and with a bullet wound to the skull, but for the most part, unharmed.

Captura! she shouted to the excited child. *Atrapar la pelota!* "Catch the ball!"

In a fit of giggles, the young girl ran on chubby legs to grab it, falling down.

Nina tonta! "Silly girl!"

Usted siempre sera mi Sueso justo! "You will always be my fair Sueso!"

The little girl giggled again, running into the arms of the nun, then to her adopted mother, as the woman lifted her up from the ground with a hug.

Dios es bueno, the good sister said, lifting her hands to the heavens. "God is good."

And indeed he was.

– – –

As Lissy was wheeled back into the jeep and the vehicle pulled away from the curb, Tha Phah, keeping a safe distance of 20 meters back, and after calling for backup, followed the truck. His men were prepared to move in the second he called the order out. As he swallowed the cold coffee down, his throat was one giant lump. Locking a clammy hand upon the wheel, he wiped the perspiration from his brow. He could hardly wait to get Rizal, and had a difficult time keeping his speed at a lawful level as he followed the jeep onto the highway. About a dozen car lengths behind the vehicle, it was critical that he maintained his anonymous profile. The girl's life was at stake, dependent upon his every move.

Trying to relieve his anxiety, his breath coming fast and loud, he popped in a CD and listened to music as he sped along, following the jeep as the highway branched into two forks, and the vehicle swerved quickly to the left, well ahead of the flow of traffic on the road. As it picked up speed, Tha Phah kept his distance. After another ten miles, the jeep merged onto another fork, and then another, leading Tha Phah through a maze of taillights and exhaust fumes. It was a warm day out, one which necessitated dark glasses, the skies above Makita City bright with sun and light with clouds. He was nervous, and kept clearing his throat, and each time he swallowed, there was a lump.

He maintained his distance of ten or twelve car lengths until the vehicle carrying Lissy turned onto another road, this one light on traffic, as he pulled back another few car lengths. When the jeep turned onto a dirt road with a Catholic church on the corner, his was the only other vehicle, which threatened the anonymity of his cover. The air was thick with the smell of potatoes and cabbage, the landscape one of dust and makeshift homes, as the jeep stopped at an ancient, metal structure surrounded by fields. As Tha Phah pulled back and slowed down, a shot rang out.

Something was wrong. Had they spotted him? Had they done away with his only witness, the girl?

Drenched in sweat, his shirt sleeves sticking to him, he called for immediate help. The jeep was now positioned diagonally to the house, and no one had gotten out. Suddenly, the metal door rolled open and a man stepped out, gun to the head of a pregnant girl.

Kumuha ng likod o kukunin ko shoot! "Get back or I'll shoot!"

This is not what he had planned at all. But it was one of the risks of the job. But he had to call off his men. He couldn't risk the life of the girl.

Placing the call, he called off his troops.

What now? Retreat? Stand his ground? Where was the girl?

Suddenly, another shot rang out, and the girl fell to the ground. In a stupor and drugged, Lissy woke to hear the gun go off and Harmony fall to the ground in a wreath of blood, bullet to her skull, the window of the jeep dripping with the ruby fluid of the *pangalawa* who had become her best friend in the *Bahay ng Biyaya*. Wide awake, her terror level on overdrive to the point that she was in danger of passing out, she fought to get out of the truck, but her feet kept her down.

50 meters in the background, Tha Phah sat frozen in his seat, in disbelief that the *traficante* had already killed a girl.

They had gunned down a girl. A pregnant girl. No respect for human life. This was the final straw. The bastards had gone too far. He would stand his ground and take them down. Someway. Somehow.

Just then, the door to the jeep opened, as Tha Phah watched Lissy being wheeled up into the house and the door rolled down behind her.

At least the girl was alive. For now.

Left with two choices, to retreat or to stand his ground, Tha Phah placed a call, this one for immediate backup, as he waited for his men to close in and surround the illegal house. He had heard of the *sanggol paggawas* or 'baby-making factories,' but had never had the 'pleasure' of being personally involved. On the rise in economically oppressed and struggling countries, the business of breeding young women for their offspring was quickly becoming a crisis across the globe, and the most despicable and horrific 'industry' of all. The money was good for the men at the top, and the *traficante de reys* and drug lords had a lucrative business, one they would not easily give up. Gunning down a pregnant *pangalawa* in cold blood was only proof of how far they would go. In quiet desperation, Tha Phah sat glued to the seat, waiting the only way he knew how. As the patrol cars swarmed upon the house, Tha Phah radioed the order to shoot on sight and to surround the house.

The filthy scumbags would not kill his girl. They would not. Neither would he let them harm anyone else.

260

Just then, the door to the jeep opened up, and a man, AK47 over a shoulder, scooped up a screaming Lissy and carried her into the house. Within a second, six patrol cars had surrounded the vehicle, guns positioned to shoot. When no one got out, they tore open the doors, but the jeep was empty. Guns upon the house, they moved steadily in. Alarmed, Tha Phah grabbed hold of the loudspeaker, his voice roaring through the air, stopping his men in their tracks.

Hold iyong sunog! "Hold your fire!" *Huwag shoot hanggang sa bigyan ako ang pagkakasunod-sunod!* "Don't shoot until I give the order!"

For the first time in his years on the force, and although he would never admit it to anyone, he was at a loss for which direction to turn. Unlike the illegal rings that he had busted up before, he had a hostage situation here. And with one, no, *two* victims dead, it was destined to get even uglier by the second. In his years of bringing the *traficantes* down, probably the most important thing that he had learned was that it was imperative to hold his ground. The *traficantes* or 'traffickers' who were holed up inside had nowhere to go but down or out, and he would smoke them out. It was a shame about Rizal though. Another no-show. And if Rizal's men were loyal to the cause, it was a possibility that they might take their own lives, taking the girls down with them in a blaze of gunfire and smoke. But before it came to that, if he felt that scenario coming down, he would call for an immediate retreat from the grounds.

Save as many lives as you can. The name of the game. That was another 'little thing' he had learned in his years in the field.

Smoke grenades. Smoke grenades would flush them out.

Without another thought to the possible implications of setting the building ablaze in a cloud of smoke, he barked the order to set off the hand grenades.

Magdingas! "Blaze!"

Left alone on the lower level and bound at the ankles, Lissy heard the glass from the second story windows come crashing down as the grenades flew through. In a cloud of yellow, the windows on the lower level were the next to go, making it impossible for her to see, and even more to breathe, the building engulfed in the yellow smoke of a half dozen hand grenades. As the windows exploded throughout the structure, another shot ran out, as Tha Phah barked another order.

Hold iyong sunog! "Hold your fire!"

As Tha Phah watched, a man ran out, arms around the neck of another very dead and pregnant girl, shouting in a choked tone that he could barely understand.

Ka shoot! Kami pumatay! "You shoot! We kill!" *Isa para sa isa, kawal batang lalaki.* "One for one, soldier boy."

The *traficante* threw the girl to the ground and started running at the same time that Tha Phah blew his head off.

Lumabas na ikaw marumi bastardo. "Take that, you dirty bastard."

He breathed a sigh of relief that the dead *pangalawa* had not been his girl.

Lissy lay on the floor of the brothel in a haze of smoke struggling to remove the rope that had been tied around her ankles. Unable to see, she pulled herself along on the floor as more shots rang out, and another dead girl was hauled out, giving Tha Phah no choice but to open fire on what had now become a full-on war. Enraged over the death of the third girl which had brought the victim count to at least six down, he shouted his orders out.

Kami ay pagpunta sa! Shoot sa paningin! "We're going in! Shoot on sight!"

In a round of rapid fire, crouching low to the ground, Tha Phah ran towards the 'house,' his firearm strapped tightly to his chest and with a dozen men behind him, as flames rose from the shattered windows onto the roof of the second floor. Now he had an entirely new problem to deal with- one of the entire structure collapsing upon itself.

How many girls were alive in the house? One? Five? Twenty? Or had they already killed them all? Had he sent his men on a suicide mission? How many men were inside? Had they taken their own lives? Was Rizal inside?

Kicking down the door through the flames and the smoke, Tha Phah hugged the floor as he made his way through the lower level amidst the sounds of screaming girls running in every which direction as his men made their way to the second floor. The smoke was so thick that he couldn't see in front of him, the yellow fumes from the grenade burning his lungs as he shouted another order, this one to the girls. The walls were ablaze and the flames were closing in, and there was no time to lose. At any second, the entire building would collapse on itself.

Kami ay sa pulis! Mabilis! Kumuha ng labas sa kaligtasan! "We are the police! Quick! Get outside to safety!"

He zigzagged through the burning building prepared to shoot on sight. There was no Rizal here, he could feel it. He was good that way, that part of his job fit him. As he ran, he stumbled over a body, hoping that it wasn't his girl. If he had to tell Lissy's parents that he had gotten this far and then had lost her... well, that was a tale that he didn't want to tell. Poised to shoot, he turned the body over, staring into what was left of the face of the dead *traficante*. The self-inflicted single bullet to the skull had done its job well, turning the trafficker's face to a pulp while blowing the rest of it off, putting the filthy scumbag out of his misery once and for all. As Tha Phah stared, the ceiling started coming down, as screaming girls ran for the staircase. As it fell, several of the girls went with it, their lives and that of their unborn offspring going up in a final hurrah of flames and smoke.

His men. His girls. He had to get everyone out. It was only a matter of seconds now.

Lahat ang na ngayon! "Everybody out now!" *Ang gusali ay bumabagsak*! "The building is falling!"

The girl! Where was his girl? If she was dead, he would never be able to forgive himself.

Yet he could no longer afford to risk his own life and remain in the house, he had to get out. Although he was not a church-going man, Tha Phah began praying like he had never prayed before, hoping that the good Lord above would hear his plea for help and that the girl with the white smile and safflower hair had been able to make it out.

As the walls collapsed in a blaze of fire and smoke, he bolted towards the door in time to see a small figure lying lifeless on the floor. Hoisting the girl upon his shoulders, he ran with her out of the burning building. Everywhere he looked girls were running blindly through the yellow fumes and smoke, hugging each other and crying, as he laid the young woman down upon the dirt. He looked at the girl and a wail rose from his chest, his tears blanketing the girl's cold nose.

It was his girl, the one he had been searching for, his Lissy.

He put an ear to her chest to see if she was breathing, but heard nothing. Performing CPR on the lifeless girl, he listened again, placing a finger upon her jugular vein, but her eyes, like his heart, were empty.

For the first time in all of the years that he had been conducting raids or *salakayins* across the country, Tha Phah broke down crying. The wail that had started out so fragile, so small, rose in decibel to that of an enraged bear as he pounded his fists upon the earth, his heart and hopes shattered. Legs shaking, he kissed the clammy forehead of the *salakayin's* latest victim, getting up from his knees just long enough to radio out for the medics who would care for the girls or *pangalawas* who had made it out alive. Grief-stricken, he surveyed his war and its damage. He had really wanted to bring the girl out alive. It was his fault that she had died. He should have retreated. He had owed it to the family. He had taken this girl's life, and the lives of almost a dozen others, and didn't even have Rizal to show for it. But, another 'small' lesson that he had learned in training was that it was never possible to save them all, but that he could always try.

War has no true survivors, only victims. Ironic, wasn't it? The 'House of Grace?' He would pray for the souls of the dead, and he would remember.

Blinded now by tears, he took a final look at what remained of the building and of the *Bahay ng Biyaya,* ashes floating midst the smolder. Such a tragedy of the loss of innocent life. The loss of his girl said it all. He would go now. His job here was finished and there was nothing else that he could do, save for shooting himself and ending it all. He owed a call to Lissy's parents.

Himalas

There are no true survivors in any war, only victims, no one emerging victorious. No engraved stone stands in memory of where Lydia lost her life that day- the cooking pots still lay in water in the bucket that served as a sink and Sueso's favorite doll still smiles at the table, and a lone sheet of bullet-ridden plywood remains. Auntie Pam, in her death of goodness and grace, was discovered lying on the kitchen floor in a puddle of dried blood three weeks after her murder, by one of the God-fearing women who had attended bible study with her at church, and who had missed seeing her sweet face at Sunday service, along with the peach cobblers that she made.

There is a thick chain that locks the iron gate where the remains of the 'soup maker's' thousands of innocent victims lay, the remains unidentifiable due to the acid that dissolved them, and to the loss of DNA. There are those who deny that claim, and who journey across the dangerous desert in a pilgrimage to pay homage to their loved one's remains. Not allowed behind the gate, they lay flowers and photographs at the entrance, tears flowing as they hug each other close and gaze sadly through the gate. It is as close as they will ever get to solving their loved one's untimely death and disappearance. And as they lay flowers in remembrance of all of the love and laughter, smiles and hugs, graduations and birthdays, another young person or innocent victim is caught within the crossfire of the drug wars, or is sold for sex or money on the streets. The *bebe fabricante* factories are still kidnapping young women throughout the nation to birth the desired *sanngols* or 'babies,' as if they are prime cuts of beef. Efforts of good men like Tha Phah are both annihilated and unrewarded, if they are even allowed in the first place. The *traficante de reys* operate a deadly and well-oiled machine.

The three *jovencitas* or young women who died in the flames on the staircase when the ceiling fell during the raid in Makita City lay buried nearby the *Bahay ng Biyaya*, in remembrance of innocence lost, a single wooden cross standing in memory. Like countless other victims of Juarez' drug wars and of the sex trades, they leave behind no known family. Eduardo's ashes lay in an urn within a vault awaiting return to his country, his grandparents saving the necessary money. Tha Phah is still working with the National Alliance of Sexually Exploited Women and Children, and has taken on another case, this one also revolving around the trafficking of underage women from the United States and the Philippines.

Trevor's parents, never accepting his death on the Ciudad, Juarez streets, visit his El Paso grave at holidays and on his birthday, when they bring chicken, soft drinks, salad, and cake, for a picnic at his grave to honor his memory. Like other wayward, addicted teens, he made the mistake of saying 'yes' to drugs and to becoming addicted, and of being in the wrong place, dying too young, too early, and without realization of his dreams. Ever since Trevor's death, his high school of El Paso reserves the first minute of every school day after the morning bell rings to honor his life and memory.

Three months after the raid on the *Bahay ng Biyaya*, Marie Boming still digs fertilizer into the soil around the morning glories, trimming them to grow even higher and stronger upon the vine as the birds flutter above them on innocent wings. In the late afternoons and when the sun is still high, their lavender shade shelters the hummingbirds as they sing. Her toil in the garden therapeutic, Marie returned to work at the gallery, and Steven to his practice as physician for a group based out of Albuquerque. Both still attend weekly addiction meetings, and recently joined a support group for families who have lost loved ones to the bloodshed at the border of Mexico and the United States.

Warm, fall evenings still find them reminiscing on the veranda in the porch swing, the escrow of the spacious, ranch home never closing. Boasting a fresh coat of paint, the For Sale sign still stands, as they sift through brochures and discuss where to put down roots as they gently laugh about days long past with Lissy. Fall has almost come and gone, the freeze of winter will soon be upon them, time to protect the trunks of the great oak trees from frost, and to lay the thick beds of straw in the barn for the animals that were birthed in the spring. Sometimes, when the time feels right, and on a breezy, fall night, and after all of the animals have been fed and housed away, they forego any discussion, choosing instead to just listen to the locusts sing, reveling in the miracle of their ability to remain motionless within the Texas earth for as many years as Lissy was in age when she became addicted to methamphetamine.

Sometimes, amidst all of the bloodshed and violence, amidst all of the greed and hate, amidst the immorality and lust and exaltation of money, in spite of the continuing drug wars and the baby-making rings, a child is saved- a frightened little girl who used to cling to her mother's hand as they walked to the marketplace in the mornings is discovered alive

60 meters from her mother's dead body, wandering the streets in which she used to play. For Sueso, every new day is a miracle of life and of new opportunity- a chance to bounce a ball, to catch a butterfly, to grow tall and strong in the protection of her adoptive parents' wings.

Not all angels fly, some come bearing gifts of song and birthday cake, and have apron strings.

And sometimes, just sometimes, in the evenings when the moon is waxing, the air is cool and the breeze blows just the right way, the doe with the scar above her eye and the speckled tail that lives beside the river comes down to the garden to drink. And sometimes, when the breeze is right, Auntie Pam stills sings.

– – –

Exhaustion can be a difficult thing, which the weary man knew as he dunked his head beneath the hose to wash off the stink. It had been a long day, the most difficult one of his life, and he wanted to forget everything and just return home to his family. He yearned to give his young wife and son a kiss, to help untie his wife's apron strings and to dry the dinner dishes, to read his son a favorite bedtime story before he went to sleep. And then at the end of the day, he wanted to close his eyes to forget once and for all the horrors that he had seen. He let the water run down upon him, its goodness cooling his face.

What was the name of that book again? The Boy and the Tree? It wasn't coming to him! Wait a minute, oh yes! The Boy Who Climbed the Olive Tree. He couldn't wait to get home so that he could read it again to his son.

As a child growing up in Brooklyn, before the birth of his son, before his marriage, there had been a tree in the family yard, just one- an apple tree, but not one that grew olives. And as a small child, he had been told how olive trees that grew too far from the sea bore no fruit, which made him wonder why they were even called olive trees. He had also heard how there were some olive trees that did bear fruit, despite their distance from the sea, and despite the fierce heat and spray used to kill the fruit flies upon them. Which made the olive tree sort of magic and special, at least in his eyes, the eyes of a father who, in the evenings, read his son to sleep after bouncing him upon his knee.

The Boy Who Climbed the Olive Tree. He would read it tonight to his son. Twice. But only after he had put on his pajamas and brushed his teeth. And after he had kissed his wife.

As he ran the cold water over his face, he heard the muffled cry of an animal not too far away. The creature sounded as if it was wounded, and, drawing his gun, he decided to investigate. The strange sound seemed to be coming from somewhere in the brush off to his left, as he crept slowly forward, gun raised. Prepared to shoot on sight if the creature tried to attack him, he walked carefully, methodically, as the animal voiced its pain to the night, and although he was a big man, he was afraid. To ease his mind, he thought about his little boy, and about the story that they liked to read, and he wondered if his son missed him, and if he was already asleep. If he was, he would certainly steal a great big hug and a kiss, being careful not to disturb his sleep. And then he would straighten the covers up around him and close the door quietly when he left.

Pulling back the trigger, he walked boldly through the weeds, closing in on the wounded creature quietly, but it was dark and he couldn't really see. It was also the middle of nowhere, and there was no one within miles. He crouched down as the animal cried again in pain, and he wondered if it was a wounded possum or a skunk, in which case he would have to put a bullet in its brain to halt its pain. And then, as if frightened by the night, the creature screamed, loud and long, as he uncovered its hiding place. He fired a shot at it which ricocheted off a rock, and pulling back the trigger again, he readied his aim. And then, in a moment that he would describe much later as a sign of God's grace, he saw that the wounded thing was a frightened girl, and he put the gun away.

Covered in dirt and soot, she lay there sobbing in the weeds as he fell to his knees.

It was his girl, his Lissy! The girl who had been erroneously listed as a 'runaway,' and who he thought had died in the flames of the Bahay ng Biyaya or House of Grace.

Right there and then, Tha Phah, who had never been a church-going man, lifted his hands to give thanks to the heavens, in praise of the *himala* or 'miracle' of life that had allowed him to stay behind to rinse himself after he had sent his men away.

Lissy? Sigurado ka okay? "Lissy? Are you okay?"

Sigurado ka nasaktan? "Are you hurt?"

Her face was bruised and her robe was torn, her safflower hair tangled, but her wide, grateful almond eyes melted his weary soul.

"I'm alright," she replied. "I just want to go home."

Her nightmare was over. She was finally going home.

Diyos ay mabuti, Tha Phah said. "God is good."

"Yes, he is," said Lissy, as Tha Phah gently untied the rope and brushed back a lock of silky hair.

With a hearty laugh, he scooped her up in his arms and carried her to the waiting jeep.

– – –

In the non-descript, yet artsy town of El Paso, like in every other community across the world that makes up the human race, there are things that change, like the names of the sophomore football players at the local high school who are picked for first string, and the semester's required textbooks for English and History. The seasons change, summer into fall, then winter into spring, as do the patients who walk in to Steven's practice, and out again. The morning glories that Marie plants faithfully every season in the garden bloom and grow, as they do every season, but their colors change.

Yet there are things in El Paso and elsewhere across the nation that never change. The waddle of baby ducks behind their mother as they walk down to the water and out again, the bleating of newborn calves each spring, the cry of an infant at birth, and the hope that we have in each other as a people, as a family, all remain. A junior at El Paso High School, Lissy is not only back in her studies, but excelling, her addiction to methamphetamine but a horror of her past, like the surrogacy that she faced, and the flames that enveloped the *Bahay ng Biyaya,* the House of Grace. Like Sueso, she was one of the lucky, a *himala* or miracle that rose from the horrors of the Mexican and Philippine trafficking and drug wars.

And then there are things which are there for our taking, if we just choose to believe. Things like love and hope and the doe that visited Lissy's great-grandmother Coral at the creek as she panned for moon dust that day. And how sand, when rubbed just the right way, turns into the moon dust of our dreams.

Like a mother's love, tucked away protectively in the trunk, their presence still strong, the small bag of sand and the letters for Lissy remain.

www.ingramcontent.com/pod-product-compliance
Lightning Source LLC
Chambersburg PA
CBHW050014180626

46810CB00002B/418